THE MALACHITE MAZE

Book II | The Ruthenian Chronicle

Rebecca Ganesh

CONTENTS

CHAPTER 1

An Old Friend

Standing tip-toe on the wooden bench, Masha gripped the window's bars and peered out into Vecherniy's slums. The wooden, thatch-roofed houses sagged into the mud; and half-dressed children ran wild through the streets while their parents labored to put food on the table or pay the landlords. She closed her eyes for a moment. She had promised herself that she would get out of the Duskhollow slum, but now the last she would see of Ruthenia would be the same mud in which she was born.

Behind her, the lock on the jail door rattled. The other women and children shrunk. Masha turned as the jailer – a portly man with one eye – and his guards entered.

"Maria Tarasovna," the jailer barked.

Her pulse caught in her throat. Few left a Vecherniy jail for better places. If your family did not scrape together the bond money, you were likely to be sold to a slaver from Skania or Nyemets or even Bolgharia and taken west or southeast to Zorya-knew-where. Even if they knew or cared where she was, Masha's parents would not spend their few coins on bringing a criminal home.

Because that was what Masha was – a criminal.

Her nails biting into her palms, Masha made herself known to the jailer. She wouldn't let another woman – or Zorya forbid, a child – take her place amongst a slaver's caravan.

"Murdered your husband, eh?" The jailor sniffed as though she were disgusting. Perhaps she was. "Well, you're off my hands now. Your bond's been bought."

Masha hung her head, certain that she would be handed over to a slaver. The guards bound her wrists and then manhandled her through the door. She blinked in the small, dim room that served as the jail's intake area. They returned nothing to her – not her apron, belt, nor knife – and shoved her towards the man who had bought her bond.

Her chest throbbed, and she thought her heart might stop. The man was towering and had hair so blonde that it might have been white – just like a Skanian. She had heard their slavers were brutes, using their slaves until they sold them for astronomical prices in slave markets all over the world. She fought back tears. She would not cower. Not now. Not when she had escaped so much. She would survive this too. Escape it. Somehow.

"Come," he said in unaccented Ruthenian, taking her by the arm.

That was when she really looked at him. White-blonde hair, gray eyes like a northern sky, full lips perpetually pressed into a firm line. She could barely breathe as he led her out of the jail. "Dir Olegovich?"

"Masha." He did not look at her.

Masha had not thought anyone could be worse than a slaver. But maybe Dir Olegovich was. "I have not seen you in–"

"I know."

Zorya's tits, he did not want to talk. Masha shouldn't want to either. But she feared that her throat would close up if she didn't keep talking. "*You* paid my bond?"

He led her out into the street and pulled her down a narrow road. "The Gray Woman Tavern is there."

Masha remembered the tavern with its mural of a woman in a gray *rubakha*, her gray hair streaming behind her. But she had never gone in. Neither she nor her parents had ever had the money to spend on ale or company. Inside, the place was dark and shabby and smelled strongly of piss. She tried not to gag.

Dir pressed her down on a squeaking bench and then straddled it.

Masha looked at him again. The last time she had seen him,

they had been teenagers. He had been just as tall but as skinny as a stalk of rye. When had he built all that muscle? And what about that scar cutting against his jaw? She closed her fingers around her skirt so she wouldn't be tempted to reach out to him.

They weren't friends anymore.

"I never thought you'd murder someone," he said under his breath.

She had never thought she'd be a murderer either. She didn't meet his gaze. "I never thought you'd be the one to pay my bond."

"I didn't either." Dir took her chin between his thumb and pointer, examining her face. His touch made her wilt, her insides aching. "But circumstances change."

They do. She remained silent as he rolled up her sleeves. What he was checking for, she wasn't certain. She was filthy; and she doubted he could see past the grime. After a moment under his examination, she said, "You can let me go now."

His lips thinned. "I'm not doing this because I pity you. I bought your bond because I need your help."

Masha stiffened. "Who said I'll help you?"

Dir lifted and dropped a shoulder. "You'll help me, or I'll tell everyone what you are."

Her hair stood on end. "A murderer?" she whispered. "They already know that."

"No."

She pressed her bound hands to her mouth. She felt sick. Of all the people in the world, Dir *knew.* In all the years that she had been gone, she had almost forgotten that. But she had been a foolish child. She had told her best friend that she saw spirits; and some of those spirits knew what she was and taught her their ways. Masha was a *ved'ma,* a witch.

"So, will you help me?" Dir asked. "Or should I return you to the jail and tell them what I know?"

Without even knowing what she was agreeing to, she said, "I'll help."

CHAPTER 2
The Beloved's Name

Masha raised her yellow *rubakha*'s skirt above the mud as Dir guided her by her shoulder through the Duskhollow slums. She wondered if her old neighbors recognized her. It had been nearly a decade. Surely she no longer looked like the young woman who had rode away on the rich farmer's wagon. Time had given her wider hips, heavier breasts, and soft lines on her brow. Her *rubakha* would have been nicer than she had ever worn before, but now it was grimy and stained from her time in prison.

"What am I helping you with?" she asked.

"Have you heard of the prize the Princess will give anyone who brings her the Pervaya Korona, the Ancestral Crown?" He steered her around a corner. "I'm going looking for that crown."

"I don't know where it is," Masha protested. "No one does."

Dir was silent as he pushed her up a flight of rickety stairs that clung to the side of a building. These looked like apartments, but they weren't where he had once lived. He unlocked the door on the second story and pushed her inside. The apartment was little more than a single room that was cramped by a table and a pair of stools, one of which was occupied by a tall man with golden blond hair. Masha spotted sleeping mats folded up in the far corner.

She had lived no better as a child, and she had truly hoped that she had escaped such spartan living. She doubted Dir planned to offer her a finer place to stay. And surely murderers did not live in luxury.

The blond man on the stool looked up from whittling a cup

from wood. "Dir, what are you doing with–?"

"I said I knew someone who could help," Dir grunted.

"Askold Olegovich," Masha said. "Do you remember me?"

Askold blinked several times. Masha had not spent much time with Askold, who was younger than Dir by eight years. He had been barely twelve when she had married and left for her husband's farm. She wouldn't recognize him, save for the uncanny resemblance between him and his brother. And she would know Dir anywhere.

"Maria Tarasovna?" Askold gripped something – a cane – and began to stand. "I thought you had a husband and a farm."

"My husband is dead." She shot a glance at Dir, wondering how many people knew what she had done. "I was brought back here."

"Sit," Dir said, pressing her onto the empty stool. She flinched when he drew his knife, but he only used it to saw at the rope around her wrist. She bit her lip in relief when the restraints fell away. Dir touched the rope burn. "I have a salve for this."

Masha hid behind small talk. "What have you been doing since I last saw you?"

"Dir and I joined the army." Askold tapped his leg with his cane. "I got a spear through my leg and couldn't fight anymore, so I whittle. Dir is a guard at a merchant's warehouse."

"You didn't take your father's spot as a Varyag?" Masha asked Dir. The Varyag were Skanian warriors who guarded the Princess of Vecherniy and high-ranking *boyars*. His father had been one.

"Dir and I aren't pureblooded Skanian," Askold answered for his brother, who was opening a jar of bitter-smelling ointment.

Masha nodded. Askold and Dir's brutish, ceiling-high father had married their mother – a soft and berry-brown-eyed Ruthenian woman.

After smearing the ointment over her burns, Dir handed her a pouch of spicy-smelling herbs. "Mix that with water – we have some in that bucket – and cover your bruises and scrapes with it."

She couldn't help herself. "Why do you care if I have bruises and scratches and ropeburn?"

"I still remember you pulling walnuts from your pockets so that you could play marbles with the rest of us," he said. "I hope that some of that child is still in you."

Masha felt hot. Her parents hadn't given her toys, instead encouraging her to make herself useful around the house or near the forge. So when the neighborhood children had taken an interest in marbles, she had needed to improvise. Masha had taken the closest thing she could find. Walnuts. They certainly weren't as durable as the stone marbles that her friends used, but she had been able to play.

Zorya's flaming tits, but was he *trying* to embarrass her? Having to poison her husband was enough humiliation. Having Dir *know* her marriage failed was enough shame for a lifetime. Now, he had to remind her how truly pathetic she had always been.

Askold watched the two of them nervously and then said, "Dir is going to find the Pervaya Korona. The Princess has offered 5,000 *grivna* for whoever can find it for her. She says that it belonged to her ancestors and it is her bloodright. You are going to help Dir?"

Masha put on a brave smile, though she doubted the crown existed at all. She suspected the Princess only wanted to create false hope for Vecherny's poorest. "I said I would help, but I don't know where it is."

"Dir does," Askold said. "Or he has a theory."

"The Copper Mountain," Dir said, sliding the burn ointment back on its shelf.

The Copper Mountain was a lone peak that stood above the fields and fenlands of Vecherniy to the southeast of the city. It was believed to be haunted, and at least a half-dozen children's stories were told of the mountain.

"Why would it be there?" Masha asked.

"Because no one has looked there," Dir said. "And because of the stories. Take the story about the Beloved's Name. The Old Ones lived on the mountain and did not understand the luxury in which they lived – fashioning needles from gold, letting their children play with gemstones.

"Eventually, the Ruthenians arrived," he continued. "When the Ruthenians realized how much wealth the Old Ones had, they decided to claim it for their own. But before the Ruthenians attacked, a kind nobleman spirited away to the Old Ones to warn them. He fell in love with the Old Ones's *kniazhna*, and she with him. He recommended that the Old Ones bury their wealth in the mountain."

"And you think among their gold was the Ancestral Crown?" Masha asked, silently wondering if that meant the crown was just as cursed as the mountain.

"Yes," said Dir.

"If the story is true," she said, "then it is protected by a ghost. The Ruthenians attacked and killed everyone – except for the *kniazhna* who used magic to seal herself and the gold into the mountain. She has protected the mountain and its treasures ever since."

Dir nodded. "The Copper Mountain is cursed because of our greed."

"And everyone who tries to find its treasure dies," she said.

"Dir will find it," Askold said quietly. "He has to."

Masha did not know whether to debate or not. The stories about the Copper Mountain might just be superstition. She knew about superstition too well: people lumped *ved'ma* in with *koldun* – demon summoners – and thought they practiced evil magic. Maybe the mountain was harmless. But she didn't want to test the theory. "Why do you need the crown?"

"I need the money," Dir said. "Askold's leg is getting worse. The stairs and the muddy roads are too much. We need to move, but we don't have the money."

"You could have asked me–" Her voice died. Of course, he couldn't. Their friendship died a decade ago. Besides, Dir would never take her husband's money. "There must be some other way."

Dir turned away and busied himself with his sword and whetstone. Masha avoided Askold's gaze. How much about their friendship's end had he told his brother? She wished that no one knew, that the entire world – including herself and Dir – could forget that she and Dir had ever known each other. That would make her life easier to bear. Alas, she would always wonder what would have happened if she had chosen differently.

CHAPTER 3

Chernava

Dir had sworn that he would never again look upon Maria Tarasovna nor speak her name. He had tried not to think about her either, but it was as if she was branded into his mind, forever a mark in his memories. And he had done so well to put her out of his life until now.

He glanced at the gray clouds hanging low overhead. Rain was coming soon, and they had another mile to go until they reached the next town. He lengthened his stride, though he kept Masha in his periphery. He would not let her sneak away. He needed her. So much that he broke his promise to himself and looked at her over and again and even said her name when he had to.

Her golden-brown hair and flushed cheeks had the same effect on him as they had ten years ago, too. His skin felt hot and too tight. He hated it.

She hugged herself. "When did your parents pass away?"

"My father during the war," he said. "My mother, last year from bloodlung."

"I'm sorry," she murmured.

"I don't want to talk about it." *Not with you.*

She was silent for several moments and then she asked, "How are my parents?"

He sucked on his teeth. "Still running their tinkering shop."

"Do they ... know what I've done?" she asked.

He nodded.

"Ah."

Her parents preferred their coin and their reputation to

their daughter. They always had – and had instilled such cold-hearted avarice into her. As a child, Dir could not fathom such lukewarm parents. Now, he did his best to not think about it. It was bad enough that he had to travel with Masha. He did not need to feel sorry for her.

They traveled in silence for the last mile to Chernava. The first village outside Vecherny, Chernava crouched like a black scab amongst lengths of farmland. The buildings were painted black with red and gray accents; and most of them stunk of moldering rushes, their thatch roofs in desperate need of repair or replacing. From what he remembered of traveling during his time in the army, the people here weren't particularly warm, but that suited Dir fine. He wasn't in a talking mood.

They stopped at Chernava's inn, partaking of *kasha* and black currant preserves. A handful of other intrepid-looking treasure hunters were also there, boasting about how they would find the Ancestral Crown. Not if Dir could help it. Across from him, Masha barely ate. Instead, she pulled at her coat as though to cover as much as her *rubakha* as possible. He frowned. The dress *was* stained, likely from her days in prison. He looked away. The prettiness of her clothes wasn't his problem. He'd already given her that coat, which had been his when he was younger, to stave off the cold.

Not to mention he'd spend three-dozen *kuna* paying off her bond.

"Upstairs," he said when he had finished and it was clear she wouldn't eat.

Bowing her head, she led the way up the stairs and then Dir ushered her into the bare-bones room he had rented. He locked the door with the key from the inside and tucked the key into his beltpurse so that she could not sneak away in the night. He removed his cloak and then began unlacing his leather breastplate.

Masha sat on her cot. He wondered how she looked beautiful even with a sullen look on her face. "You have a tear in your cloak."

Dir lifted the item and found the rip just above the elbow. Sighing, he rummaged in his pocket for his sewing kit.

She held out her hands. "Let me."

His fingers tightened around the fabric. He did not need her touching his things, making her mark. Not to mention, it cut to be reminded that he couldn't afford something as simple as a seamstress. Was Masha doing this on purpose, just to prove the point she'd made a decade ago?

"I know your mother did not teach you," she said. "I will do it."

Biting the inside of his cheek, Dir let her take the sewing kit and cloak. She threaded the needle and made small, even stitches. Just like any other woman would have. It was so mundane. So why did he want to watch her mend for hours?

"When we were younger," she said, "you liked to hear about the house spirits I saw. About the *kikimora* that taught me my runes. I can tell you one of those stories."

Dir tensed as he set aside his breastplate and bracers. "I don't want to hear your stories."

"You know, I didn't mean– I should have refused to see you," she said. "My parents told me not to. Maybe if I had listened to them, maybe if I had waited, then I wouldn't have said such–"

"Don't." His ears burned. "What's done is done. There is no point in talking about it."

He lay on his lumpy, stale-smelling cot and glared at the ceiling. It was better than looking at her. If there was any other way of getting the Pervaya Korona, he would have done it. But Masha was the only person he knew who could charm spirits and use magic. And for a vengeful spirit like the girl in the Copper Mountain, he needed all the help he could get.

After a while, Masha set his folded cloak at the end of the cot. He refused to look.

CHAPTER 4
Ruined

After Chernava, Dir tried to enforce silent travel. No matter what Masha said, he became angry. And he was tired of being angry at her. He had been angry at her for a decade. Her presence only opened up old wounds. Still, she tried to mend what she had burned to ash years ago.

"Do you still like lingonberries?" she asked. "I know your mother had a bush in front of your old apartment."

Dir did not answer, only walking a little faster. How was the woman he hated most in the world also the woman who knew the most about him?

"If we slow down, we will spot a lingonberry bush," she said.

"I need to get back to Askold," he said.

Even from here, the Copper Mountain stood like a sleeping giant on the southern horizon, blanketed in a fine mist. He always kept it in his sight and in his mind. The Pervaya Korona *had* to be there. He *had* to get the crown so he could get the promised silver and get Askold out of the slums. And prove to everyone that he would not remain poor forever.

"Maybe in a larger town, a baker will have lingonberry pies," Masha suggested. "Or a wife will be selling lingonberry preserves."

He turned to her. "What is *so* important about lingonberries?"

She shrunk back, her voice quiet. "I thought it would make you ... happier."

Dir grimaced and turned back to the road. He hadn't meant to be so gruff, nor did he want her to flinch when he looked at her.

He clenched and unclenched his fists. If he could just focus on the task at hand and not Masha, he would not be so frustrated.

An arrow whistled past his ear.

He grabbed Masha, hauling her behind him as another arrow struck the ground where she stood. From the bushes below the road, shadows took shape. Bandits. Dir drew his sword as the vagabonds clambered up the slope like wildcats.

"Fancy yerself a fighter?" said a bandit with two missing front teeth. His comrades drew their own nasty-looking blades and fanned out. "Give us the whore and yer silver and we'll let y'live."

Dir's time fighting Nyemetsky during the war taught him: he who strikes first lives. He charged, his sword slashing across the first bandit's chest. The toothless man fell. Dir cut towards another, and the sword clipped the man's neck. He spun and blocked an attack from a mangy-looking woman. He elbowed her back. Then shoved his sword through her belly.

He only realized Masha was behind him when there was a tug on his belt. She took his belt knife and thrust it into the soft spot under the final bandit's arm. The man's eyes glazed over, his knees buckled, and then he collapsed.

Dir stared at Masha, processing what she had done. Stolen his knife to kill the bandit rushing him from behind. "You saved me."

"They wanted to hurt me. You haven't hurt me" – her voice dropped – "yet."

Yet, he echoed silently, cleaning his sword on one of the bandit's cloaks before sheathing it. Quietly, he said, "I don't plan on hurting you."

She stepped closer as he pulled his knife from the bandit's armpit. She touched his arm, and he flinched. "You're hurt."

It was only then that he felt the throb in his arm. A clean laceration cut across his upper arm and leaked red-black blood onto his sleeve and down his bracer. He grimaced.

"Let me help you," Masha said. "Do you have an apple or a stone fruit in your pack?

Dir shook his head. He remembered her healing spell: Masha carved runes into an apple and then had her patient eat it. She had healed his broken nose that way. "I don't need your magic."

"My magic is better than letting you bleed out."

Again, she took the belt knife from him. Pushing back the shorn edges of his sleeve, she found unblemished skin and then pressed the tip into his flesh. Dir cursed, and she told him to hold still. The rune she carved in his upper arm was jagged and bloody, but when it was done, it glowed a faint orange before mending along with the laceration from the bandits.

Masha stepped back, silent. Strands of her golden-brown hair stuck to her face, and her brown eyes watched him almost warily. The urge to touch her was suddenly overwhelming.

He opened and closed his fingers, causing his still-healing arm to throb. The feeling was better than wanting to touch Masha.

"Come on," he said. "I don't want to explain why there are four corpses here. And we need to keep going."

As they walked southward, the sky grew dark with low-hanging clouds; and soon it began to rain. The drizzle rolled off his cloak and her coat, but as the rain turned to a deluge, the waterproofing began to fail. Dir searched the horizon for shelter. Eventually, amongst the endless grazing fields and strips of farmable land, he spotted a granary. Propped up on stilts to protect the grain from vermin, the granary was only half-standing. Time and weather had collapsed its eastern side; and some large bird had built – and then abandoned – its nest there. It wasn't the most comfortable shelter, but it was better than walking the rest of the day and night in the rain.

Inside, he used old hay and barley stalks for kindling, coaxing a small fire that charred the floor to life. Then, from his pack, he rationed out a handful of dried currant, a slice of hard cheese, and a slice of stale horsebread for himself and Masha. Silently, he worried about having enough coins to fund this entire excursion. He had to make every meal and every *kuna* stretch.

Masha hugged her knees to her chest, her skirt revealing her ankles and the bottom of her shapely calves. "Dir, I've regretted what I said–"

"I don't want to talk about it."

"Please, listen," she said.

He closed his eyes. *Fine.*

"I have regretted what I said ... that day ... for the past ten years," she said.

He saw Masha – much younger – in her best *rubakha* with the neckline newly embroidered and her mother's good *panova* layered on top. His younger self had thought she was so beautiful and wished that she had been dressed that way for him. He wished he could carve the memory out of his mind.

"My parents wanted me to marry Gennadiy Borisovich," she said. "They told me not to talk to you, not to see you. They didn't want my groom to think you had ... ruined ... me."

"Ruined," Dir echoed. Zorya's teeth, he had wanted her. But he would have waited. Waited until he married her. Waited until she was ready. Waited until she wanted him, too.

"He was giving them a bride price," she continued. "He had a profitable farm and savings. My parents promised me I would never be sad, never be hungry, never be hurt – that his money would fix everything."

Dir made a sound somewhere between a wheeze and a laugh. "What a perfect man."

"Yes, a perfect man," she murmured bitterly. Then, she continued, "I believed them. I shouldn't have."

"You told me I was poor and always would be." Dir scrubbed at his face. "That I could never take care of you."

"Dir, you were my best friend. I didn't know you–" *Loved you,* he thought as she struggled to find the words. "That you felt that way about me. I didn't know how to say no. So, I just gave the reason my parents kept saying."

He felt like someone had put a sword through his heart. He stood up. "That makes it worse. They said that about me and you *believed* them?"

Masha inched back, and Dir stilled.

"I frighten you," he said softly.

"No," she said, too strongly. "You don't frighten me."

He moved away from the fire, sitting with his back against the wall. He had meant what he said: he didn't want to hurt her. Even if she had ripped open a wound that wouldn't heal all those years ago. He didn't want to frighten her either. But he did. He resolved to rein in his anger – or at least hide it better.

Close to the fire, Masha finally turned to her food.

CHAPTER 5

Ovinnik

Dir woke to his breath curling silver in the bitterly cold air and the sound of rain on the granary's roof. The fire had long sputtered out. Across from its ashes, Masha lay curled on the floor, sleeping fitfully. Her braid was half undone, making her look more youthful and carefree than she was. For a long moment, he struggled with the desire to stroke her hair. Eventually, though, he managed to focus on himself. He had fallen asleep sitting up, and his neck ached badly. He rubbed his neck, rolling his shoulders.

In the dark, something moved.

On his feet, he drew his knife and then moved quickly across the room. He gripped Masha's shoulder. "Shh, something's wrong."

Then he heard it: a hiss, like a match being struck. A pair of orange-red eyes peered out of the dark. Around the eyes emerged a cat-like face with a beard and bushy brows made from twisted straw. Then, its skeletal and human-esque body came into view.

"An *ovinnik*," Masha murmured just as Dir's hairs stood on end.

"You trespass on my home," the spirit hissed, "and draw a blade on me."

Masha gripped his knife hand, but Dir pulled away from her.

"I should set fire to the barn and burn you inside it," the *ovinnik* said. "But I will be merciful. Answer my riddle and I will let you stay the rest of the night. Fail and I will cast you out."

"We'll answer your riddle," Masha blurted before Dir could say anything.

The *ovinnik* smiled, revealing silver and needle-like teeth, and then built its puzzle.

> *"A slight forgotten,*
> *A friend kept close,*
> *A regretful occurrence,*
> *But what matters most.*
> *What am I?"*

Beside him, Masha was repeating the riddle under her breath. Dir shifted the knife in his hand, his anger turning white-hot. He was not here to let Masha play games with wayward spirits. Sensing Dir's thoughts, the *ovinnik*'s smile vanished, its eyes glowing like burning coals.

"I'm still thinking," Masha said.

Dir stalked towards the spirit, which hissed and arched its back like a cat.

"Dir, wait," Masha said. "I know the answer!"

He slashed at the *ovinnik* with his knife.

But he didn't hit his mark.

Instead, he stood in the middle of the road, icy rain pelting him. At his feet, Masha sat on the ground, her surprise painted on her face. He offered his hand, glancing around for signs of his pack. He spotted it a few feet away. The half-collapsed granary was gone. Vanished.

"I had the answer." She wiped rainwater from her face. "We could have stayed the night."

"We didn't know what it wanted," he grumbled. "Or what it would actually do if your answer was wrong."

"It was just playing with us." She stood without his help. "You didn't need to attack it."

Dir looked away from her. He was hot beneath his collar, even as the rain soaked him to the skin. He would not get into an argument with her right now. Whatever frightened her about him would only be magnified by the night and the rain. And he could not afford her fleeing.

"You'll have plenty of time to play games with the spirits inside the Copper Mountain," he said. "Forget the minor ones on the road."

He continued down the road, the rain filling his boots, and Masha – thank Zorya – followed closely. As he sought another shelter – however measly – he considered Masha's past. She had always turned to the household spirits for company and guidance. He hadn't thought much of it back then, his childlike innocence simply taking her at face value. By the time he was a teenager, he was used to her stories of the *kikimora* in the kitchen and the *dvorovoy* who lived in the garden. Perhaps she had played games with them and so it was not so strange to answer an *ovinnik*'s riddles.

Dir shook his head. Remembering her fanciful stories only made him nostalgic. And his nostalgia hurt. He put those memories away.

"There's a tree," he said. "We can shelter under its branches the rest of the night."

As he climbed off the road and into the tree's roots, Dir realized the toll that the weather took on Masha. She hugged herself and visibly shuddered from the cold, her lips tinged blue. When he helped her down into the shallow divot that the tree made, he noticed how her *rubakha* and coat were heavy from the rain. He stripped his breastplate and then grabbed Masha by the shoulders. Her eyes widened as he peeled her coat from her shoulders, casting it aside. He guided her to a dry spot on the ground and then, lying behind her, drew her firmly against her chest. Over them both, he draped his cloak.

Dir bit back a curse. Touching her was wrong. After ten years, she was almost a stranger to him. And if she wasn't, she was the last person in the world he should hold. He told himself that, if he didn't need her help to get the Ancestral Crown, he wouldn't have helped her. But that was a lie. No matter how much he hated her, he wouldn't let Masha die. Not if he could help it.

He stared at the brown leaves clinging to the branches above. If he had to touch Masha to keep her warm, it didn't mean he had to look at her. Maybe he could forget that the soft body beside him was the woman he had once wanted more than anything.

"When I was seven or eight," Masha began, "Irinushka and Verochka cornered me in an alley. I remember they had these large scissors, like for cutting wool. They told me they would shear me like a sheep. Verochka had me by the hair, and Irinushka was opening and closing those scissors in front of my face.

"That's when you came," she continued. "You were ten or eleven maybe. You took the scissors and bent them and then chased Irinushka and Verochka off. I think I was crying. You helped me up and helped me braid my hair."

His fingers tightened. He was holding her upper arm. He forced himself not to look down at her. He remembered that day. A normal father would have striped his hide for destroying the scissors, but his Skanian father simply told Irinuskha's mother that the girl shouldn't wield a sword she wasn't prepared to shatter on an enemy shield. Dir would have taken the beating, if it meant protecting Masha.

"I know you defended the other children too," she said. "You were always a protector. Always helping those who needed it."

"What are you talking about?" he rasped.

"I know you hate me," she said, "but you are still helping me."

Dir didn't respond, and they fell into an awkward silence. Eventually, though, his curiosity won out. "Masha, what was the answer to the *ovinnik*'s riddle?"

"It doesn't matter anymore."

CHAPTER 6

Slomaniy

Though she was sore and cold and had walked for hours to reach the town of Slomaniy, Masha could think of nothing but the feel of Dir against her back. That rye stalk of a boy was now a man made of muscle and sinew. Under no circumstances should she allow another man into her life – not after her disastrous marriage to Gennadiy – but that did not mean that her nerves were not on fire from a night spent against him. She touched her throat, looking at everything but the broad-shouldered man ahead of her.

Long ago, the village of Slomaniy had planted oak trees to block the wind that cut across the heath. The trees grew large, their canopies blocking out the sun and their roots growing up through the roads. And their roots dug deep into the Zeleny River, siphoning water, and stretched beneath the roads, causing them to buckle.

"That looks like an inn," Dir said.

Memories of sleeping against a muscled body flooded her. *I murdered my husband,* Masha reminded herself as she followed him into the inn.

The Red Rabbit Inn was bursting at the seams. Squeezing into the inn's dining hall, Masha found a new reason to admire Dir's intimidating height and bulk: his presence made the crowds give way. Dir strode easily through the mass of people partaking of *pelmeni* and *kvass*, towards the center of the establishment where an auburn-haired woman leaned against the bar.

The woman gave Dir a warm, appraising look that made Masha's stomach harden. "You poor man, out in the cold." The woman brought a stool. Only one. "Sit, sit."

Dir gestured for Masha to sit. She did without protest. She was too tired and too cold to fight right now; and resting her legs felt too good. The innkeeper barely acknowledged that Masha was there, instead handing Dir a steaming cup of *kvass*. For Masha, she had nothing. Again, Dir offered the *kvass* to Masha first; and again, she didn't refuse. It was only then that the innkeeper narrowed her eyes at Masha.

The innkeeper ladled another mug of hot *kvass* for Dir and asked him about his travels. "Another treasure hunter?"

Dir lifted and dropped a shoulder. "The Princess offers a pretty price."

The innkeeper touched his arm, her voice soft and sweet. "You look like you have plenty of … experience. I'm sure you will be luckier than most."

Masha knocked her boot against the bar, but no one noticed.

"You must miss the comforts of Vecherny," the innkeeper was saying. "A soft bed, fresh bread, good company…"

Propping her cheek on her fist, Masha stared into her *kvass*. It smelled like rye and black currant with a hint of cinnamon. She felt … invisible.

Of course, women liked Dir. He was dedicated and loyal and strong and built like a soldier. He didn't have to hide the fact that he talked to spirits and practiced magic. He didn't parrot his parents' greed. He hadn't murdered his spouse.

Masha was the monster and Dir the hero.

Maybe, though, she wanted someone to speak gently to her. Even if it was lunacy to want it. She remembered too well how her husband Gennadiy's concern turned to cruelty so easily, twisting her every emotion to make her break quicker. She would let no one manipulate her like that again. And no matter how nice Dir felt, he would never be the one to comfort her. She had already ruined their relationship. Maybe it was for the best. So Dir would not manipulate her and she could always remember the way he was when they were young.

Masha stood and tapped the innkeeper on the shoulder. "I'm

tired. Do you have an available room?"

"I..." The innkeeper pulled a key off her ring. "The attic is still available."

Masha took the key and didn't thank her, setting off for the stairs. If Dir noticed that she had gone, he didn't come to find her. So, she let herself into the attic and settled amongst the storage boxes, trying to block as many drafts as possible. After nights on the road, she had been looking forward to a night on a pallet or cot – with a pillow. Alas, it wasn't to be. Leaning against a crate, she closed her eyes and tried to think about something pleasant – but failed repeatedly.

Instead, memories of Gennadiy's moodswings, his insults, and his hands around her throat swallowed her.

She lost track of time, so she didn't know how long she had sat alone. But eventually, Dir arrived, a bedroll under each arm. And she didn't have to think about her dead husband anymore. Dir tossed her a bedroll and spread out his. Then, he sat, cleaning his sword.

"The innkeeper likes you," Masha said.

Dir blinked. "What?"

"It would be easier to marry her, move Askold out here," she said, "than try to wrest a treasure away from that cursed mountain."

His expression darkened. "I won't marry."

"You are being stubborn," she said.

"Says the woman who only cares about silver."

Her nails dug into the bedroll as she leaned forward. "I'm not *that* greedy."

"Fine, you just parrot back what your parents say," Dir growled. "And *they're* greedy."

"I'm not that meek little girl anymore." When he shook his head in disbelief, she blurted, "I killed my husband, Dir. Do you want to know why?"

Dir turned a shade paler. This was the first time Masha had ever seen him scared. His voice was brittle. "I don't want to hear anything about that bastard you married."

"Do you think someone made me do it?" Masha pressed. "Did they put the poison in my hand? Did they make me mix it with his *shchi*?"

"Enough, Masha," he growled.

Frustration curled around her throat. He thought she was just a puppet. She would show him. "Did they make me watch him twitch on the floor as he choked?"

"Masha!" He crossed the distance between them, on his knees. "I said enough."

When he closed his hands on her shoulders, her heart plummeted. She saw Gennadiy, felt him shove her against the wall and crush her face into the wood paneling. She forced herself to breathe. Dir was just touching her, firmly but gently. She didn't need to panic.

"I believe you." He drew his hands away. "You killed him in cold blood."

In self-defense, Masha wanted to say, but her voice refused to come. Ducking her head, she began hastily unfurling her bedroll.

"I wouldn't blame you if you had," he said. "I was jealous of that bastard for years."

She couldn't look up. When Dir had come to her hours before her wedding, she hadn't expected him to ask her to abandon her groom and marry him instead. He had never once indicated that he wanted her that way. So, she turned him down, and when he insisted, she echoed her parents' fears about money.

For years, suffering under Gennadiy's fists, she wondered what would have happened if she had accepted Dir's suit instead.

"I eventually accepted that you weren't worth it," he murmured, returning to his bedroll.

Not worth it. She bit her lower lip. *That* was why her parents never came to help her, why her father-in-law allowed Gennadiy's to beat her, why her neighbors never intervened. Because she was not worth it.

She lay on her bedroll with her back facing Dir and scrubbed her stinging eyes.

CHAPTER 7

Kuma Lisa

D ir's neck and shoulders hurt. It was what he got for being tense all night. Masha had wanted to give him the gruesome details of her husband Gennadiy Borisovich's death. She poisoned his food and watched him choke to death. She was right: she wasn't that meek girl he remembered anymore. He hadn't wanted to think about the ways the world had made her brutal, but those thoughts had kept him up for hours.

Masha sulked behind him, pulling her borrowed coat tightly about her. Clearly, she hadn't slept well either.

As they strode beneath the oak branches that sheltered Slomaniy's streets, Dir noticed a pair of *naalbinding* gloves embroidered with bright orange arctic poppies. Glancing back at Masha, he paid the vendor for the gloves and tucked them in his pocket. He continued on, restocking their food supplies.

A storyteller sat on the side of the road, a dozen or more children crowding her skirts as she told the story of Vasilisa the Wise. Dir felt a soft pain above his heart. He remembered gathering around the travelling storyteller as a child, listening to tales of great knights and clever maidens. Masha would have been there with him, listening to the same stories.

"Do you remember being like that?" he asked. "Listening to the storyteller?"

She did not answer immediately.

"I think your favorite was The Maiden Princess," he said.

She shook her head. "My second favorite. My favorite was The Silver Slipper."

"Do you remember mine?" he asked.

"The Princess Who Never Smiled," she said, the corner of her mouth twitching.

Dir sighed. He felt empty. That fateful day – when he had mustered all his courage and told Masha how he truly felt about her – she derided his poverty and married another man. He had lost his best friend that day. And just because this woman looked like his best friend and held all her memories, it didn't mean she *was* his best friend. That girl was gone. Masha had admitted it herself. Maybe, the girl hadn't existed at all.

He reached into his pocket and then presented her the gloves. "You looked cold. I thought these would help."

She took them, slipping them onto her hands. She said simply, "Thank you."

"I think they're Skanian-made," he said. "My grandmother used to do *naalbinding* all the time."

Masha flexed her fingers. "I always wished my family was like yours."

It was his turn to be silent.

"Your mother, father, and grandmother loved you and Askold," she said.

Dir remembered Masha – as a little girl – playing marbles with walnuts. When their gang had turned to hoops and sticks, she had pulled branches off of trees, bending them into lopsided hoops so that she could play. And rather than chalk, she used charcoal to draw out hopscotch patterns on the street. He bit the inside of his cheek. Why had he not seen what was right in front of him?

He reached out and then stopped himself. "You were not a waste of coin, Masha."

"I don't need your pity," she said.

"I do not pity you."

He watched the oak trees give way to gray sky and flurries of snow. Today's journey would be unpleasant. He set out from the town of Slomaniy. Masha kept looking over her shoulder, but when he asked what she was looking for, she brushed him off. He decided it wasn't worth the fight and didn't mention it again.

Not too far from the town, they came upon a burnt pyre. Black and charred, it was difficult to tell what it was at first, but Masha's sudden stillness gave him his first clue. When he looked closer, he noticed scraps of reed-green fabric amongst the ash. An iron brooch glinted atop a twisted, ashen shape. A woman, or what was left of a woman. Dir put a hand on Masha's shoulder.

"A witch hunter found her," Masha murmured.

"This is at least a few day's old," Dir said, feeling useless. "The witch hunter will have moved on. You're safe. I will keep you safe."

He steered her away from the violent scene.

After they had left behind the burned *ved'ma*, a serf offered them a ride on his wagon; and so Dir and Masha rolled southeastward past fields that incubated winter rye beneath a dusting of snow. Just after midday, they parted ways with the serf, who headed west towards his hamlet. On the horizon, the Copper Mountain loomed closer and closer. It might only take another day or so to reach its base. But as the snow began collecting on the road, slowing Dir and Masha to an almost unbearable pace, Dir began looking for a place to take cover.

To the east appeared an ancient brick chapel. As the sun set behind the stormclouds, Dir and Masha approached it. Tinted glass layered between the bricks formed a mural, of sorts, of the sun and the stars – with the evening star, named for Zorya, prominent. Behind him, Masha sighed. Dir agreed: he was tired and he did not want to sleep in the snow. Inside, whitewashed walls sheltered an idol that was so old it looked little more than a strangely-formed piece of wood. Dir did not like the fact that the idol reminded him of the dead *ved'ma* on the pyre.

He approached the idol. To Zorya, he offered a *kuna* for her shelter.

"Another treasure hunter?" A woman in a faded red habit approached, her cowl drawn up. She wore a bow and quiver upon her back and a long knife at her hip.

Dir let go of his sword. He was lucky he hadn't drawn it.

The nuns of Zorya's Order were warriors, every last one of them. "We're just seeking shelter for the night, Sister."

"Zorya provides shelter to all those who seek victory," the nun said, drawing back her hood.

Masha gasped and gripped his arm. "A *vila*."

The air around the nun shimmered. When he looked closer, he saw not a woman in the red habit of a nun, but something else entirely. Behind her glamour, Sister Lisa was sinewy and elongated, her eyes the shape and color of a fox's. And she wore a velvet green gown trimmed in gold, a foxskin cloak around her shoulders.

Vili were female spirits that were at home in the forest, rivers, or air. They ran in packs and were renowned warriors. They also loved to dance and take human soldiers as their lovers. Dir had never seen one before.

Again, he reached for his sword.

Masha stopped him, her hand on his wrist, her fingers tight and sure. His throat constricted as he realized that he wanted her to touch him more.

The *vila* smiled, and she had the teeth of a fox as well. "Careful, soldier. If I do not strike you dead on the first blow, Tomila will have your head before you can draw blood."

Dir started again. From the shadows, a nun as tall and broad as a man emerged. A stripe of gray through her dark hair, she glowered at him and gripped the hilt of her battleax.

Masha tightened her grip on his wrist, watching him. He could almost hear her thinking. *Trust me.*

Dir looked between the three women and then nodded minutely to Masha. She knew more about spirits than he; and he had failed with the *ovinnik*.

"I am Masha and this is Dir," she said, her voice wavering slightly.

"A polite one." The *vila* grinned, gesturing. "I am Lisa and this is Sister Tomila."

"What is a *vila* doing in a nunnery?" Masha asked.

"Sit," Lisa said. "And I will tell you."

Awkwardly, Dir sat on the floor and Masha joined him, her knee knocking against his. He couldn't quite believe that he was going to sit around the skirts of this *vila* like children did to a storyteller, but if it kept them safe and warm, he would do it.

"The Lord of Gomel wanted a lucky bride, and foxes are lucky," the *vila* began. "He spotted me while I was bathing and had left my clothes on a nearby log. He stole my cloak, which allows me to transform into a fox, and then trapped me. I lived for many years as his wife and bore him children, all while I sought to find a way to escape."

He curled his fists on his thighs. There were half-*vila* children running amok? He glanced at Masha and then away. What strange magic would a half-*vila* have?

"I had all but given up when my husband hired my Tomila as an armsmaster," said the *vila*, Lisa. "She is a *ved'ma*. And she can see spirits even if they are hidden.

"My Tomila didn't know she was a *ved'ma*, of course. I think she might have turned herself in to be burned if she knew. She only knew I wasn't what I seemed. And she is as curious as a cat and persistent as a hound."

Tomila arched an eyebrow. She was a large woman – nearly as tall and broad as him – with streaks of silver in her dark hair. "Go on."

"My Tomila tried to sniff me out," Lisa said. "In doing so, she found my foxskin cloak. My delightful husband had hidden it in his family's crypt. That was when she knew what I was: a spirit, not a woman. I filched the cloak off her and ran."

"I ran after her," Tomila said. "I thought she had stolen from the *boyar*."

"She came around though." Lisa took Tomila's hand in a way that spoke of long, quiet years together. "In the end, she brought me home to my sisters. But I could never leave my Tomila. So we are here, where the Lord of Gomel will not find us."

"As Lisa said, Zorya provides shelter to all who seek victory," said Tomila.

Angling her face away, Masha brushed a tear from her

cheek. Dir wanted to ask what was wrong, but he sensed this wasn't the time.

The *vila* noticed Masha's tears as well, her expression growing solemn. "We all hope to escape in the end."

Masha nodded and said nothing.

Dir scowled.

The *vila* twisted her wrist and a shining, silver dagger materialized in her hand. She passed it to Masha. "Take this. It can carve what nothing else can carve."

The hairs on the back of Dir's neck stood on end. "What does that mean?"

Lisa growled like an animal, her eyes flashing. "Do not concern yourself, man."

"I can use magic in places I couldn't before," Masha explained quickly.

Dir shifted uneasily. He had not given Masha a knife for two reasons: first, so she would not stab him in the back; and second, so that she could not wield magic without his approval. But as the *vila* stared him down, he felt ashamed of himself.

CHAPTER 8
The Silver Dagger

After a night sleeping on the chapel's old stone floor, Masha woke with a kink in her neck and a sore back. She kneaded her muscles, trying to remember the details of her dreams. She swore she had had a nightmare about being followed, about a witch hunter. She shook her head and told herself not to put frightening ideas into her own head. After all these nights on the road, she almost missed her bed on the farm. She tasted bile and swallowed. She had shared that cot with Gennadiy. She should be grateful to sleep wherever he was not.

Dir was already up, sharpening one of his knives. When he noticed her watching him from the corner of his eye, he sheathed the knife, stood, and then crossed the distance between them.

He offered his hand. "Up."

Licking her lips, she took his hand. It was callused and hard like the rest of him. Her heart stuttered traitorously, and she quickly reminded herself that he hated her. Unfortunately, she still remembered all too vividly sleeping with her back pressed against his chest. She prayed every night that she would forget that.

"Draw your knife," he said.

Letting go of his hand, she did. The silver knife glittered in the pale morning light. She shifted her fingers on the soft leather wrapped around its handle, watching Dir.

"If I grab you" – with his left fist, he took a handful of her coat – "use it to pierce me." With his right hand, he took her knife-hand and pressed the blade at the crux of his elbow, the blade's tip piercing his sleeve. "Like this." He pressed it to the underside of his forearm. "Or this."

"You want me to stab you?" Her voice was high and breathy as her muscles froze. How often had Gennadiy grabbed her? Pulled her by her hair or clothes so he could hit her?

"I want you to fight if you need to," he said, guiding her hand and the blade in a circular motion around his arm. "You can slice me like this."

She stared up at Dir, her blade's tip resting at the crux of his arm. He had a hold of her like Gennadiy had so many times before he struck her. But with her blade like this, Masha could disable Dir in one stroke. She had never had Gennadiy so vulnerable.

Masha dropped the knife. It clattered on the stone floor.

And immediately, Dir let her go.

She shook her head, her pulse thrumming inside her skull.

"We will practice." Slowly, he bent down, picked up the knife, and then offered it to her. "And I will teach you."

She took the knife quickly and sheathed it. He stood so close that she could smell his leather and soap. Her small hairs stood on end. He wanted to teach her how to fight? Zorya, he had pressed a naked blade to his own arm! If she had flinched, she could have maimed him. She wasn't sure if he was insane.

"Why?" she stammered.

He was quiet for a moment and then said, "When the *vila* gave you that blade, I realized I was being selfish. I was protecting myself. But you need to be able to defend yourself, too." He paused. "Probably more than I do."

Masha didn't know what to say. Her parents hadn't wanted her to fight back. Gennadiy certainly didn't. Masha had spent her entire life avoiding lashings from tongues and belts. And now Dir would put a blade in her hand and let her cut him. Her chest ached, and she didn't know how to feel.

"I also brought you along for your magic." He shrugged one shoulder. "I ought to let you use it."

"Dir…" She shook her head. "Thank you."

"If we can get the Ancestral Crown, it'll be me thanking you."

Masha was spared from responding when Sister Tomila and the *vila* Lisa arrived in the chapel. Lisa grinned mischievously, flashing pointed teeth that seemed a bit too small for a human mouth, and gestured towards the door. "Tomila has a parting gift for you."

They all exited the chapel. The sky was blue, over a field of thin, powdery snow. A white horse, whose coat glimmered in the sunlight, stood without lead or restraint as though called by magic. Perhaps it had been, thought Masha, because surely the *vila* could summon animals. Around its feet were poles – four white, four red. Tomila stepped forward, murmuring prayers to the goddess Zorya. The horse crossed the grid once, twice ... four times. It stepped gingerly and with high knees, purposefully evading the poles. Then, Sister Tomila blew in its nose and the beast cantered away, disappearing into the endless fields.

"Zorya has spoken," Tomila said. "Your path is complex and difficult to navigate, but if you step like the horse – precisely and making no wrong move – you will be certain of victory."

Dir let out a long exhale. "It's there."

Tomila nodded. "The treasure you seek is in that mountain. But be careful: no one has survived the maze yet."

"A maze?" Masha repeated, dumbfounded that Dir was *right*. That haunted mountain held the Pervaya Korona and no one else had gone looking there.

The nun gestured to the poles. "I see a maze in the way the poles fell, in the way the horse walked. But I don't know any more."

"A maze inside the mountain," Dir murmured. "It's more than I knew before."

Lisa took Tomila's hand. "With a silver dagger and knowledge of how to proceed, go. The weather will hold today, and you can reach the mountain if you do not tarry."

CHAPTER 9

Nunshood

J ust as the nun predicted, the sky remained blue and cloudless well into the afternoon as they trekked closer and closer to the Copper Mountain. At the mountain's base, Dir brought Masha into the town of Medny, where the townspeople worked a coppermine – large pitmines – just below the mountain's northern slope. Black smoke curled from the town's chimneys; and the buildings themselves were covered from ground to roof in black soot. On one side of the town, ramshackle cottages house the miners; the other side of town held the mineworks and the smelters. Dir thought the place was miserable.

But this was the end of the road, he told himself. In that mountain, its brown mass looming above him, was the Ancestral Crown. With that treasure, he and Askold could move out of Vecherniy's slums.

He remembered the words that the *vila* had said, his gaze drifting to Masha. *We all hope to escape in the end.* He and Askold were trying to escape their poverty. What was Masha trying to escape?

The thought followed him into the sinisterly-named Bloodmine Inn, so when he and Masha were alone in their sooty and spartan room, he said, "I'll give you a share of the *grivna*. You can head to Beluvod. They don't persecute *ved'ma* or other magic people there."

It's what she wanted: silver. It's why she had married Gennadiy. It was why she hadn't married him. With the Pervaya Korona, he could finally give Masha what she had always wanted. Why he still wanted to, he didn't know. But he did.

Masha was quiet for a long moment. Then, she said, "How do you know that? About Beluvod?"

"Being a guard for a merchant has taken me many places," he said. "The Prince of Beluvod's sons is a *volkhv*."

"A royal *volkhv*," Masha murmured, her voice tinged with awe. "I'd like to see that."

"Maybe you will."

Nodding, she took off her coat. Her *rubakha* showed new and old stains, and was threadbare at the hems.

Dir sighed, setting his pack on the floor. Ever since the *vila* had shamed him for protecting himself and leaving Masha at the mercy of whatever person or creature came along, he could no longer ignore the small details. Yes, he had bought her gloves, but she lacked a kerchief or cap; and her *rubakha* and coat were threadbare at best. Alas, Dir's coins were dwindling and he did not have enough money to buy her new clothes.

He bit the side of his tongue. *You don't have enough money to take care of me,* Masha had said all those years ago – and she had been right.

To distract himself, he offered to teach her to fight with her new dagger.

"You make me spar with a real blade," she said. "I could hurt you at any time."

"You haven't." He adjusted his belt around his hips. "Why not? I know you do not want to help me. So why not dig your knife into me and run?"

She visibly swallowed as she tucked her dagger away. Dir could not help but let himself admire the curve of her waist and the rosiness in her cheeks. The urge to touch her – that he had long suppressed – burned his palms. He closed his fists and kept them firmly at his sides.

"Maybe I just remember that skinny boy who was my friend," Masha replied quietly.

He sighed. Zorya's teeth, but she knew how to cut him deep. "What do you remember about that skinny boy?"

"He broke branches off of trees and tried to teach me and

Askold how to fight with swords." She laughed softly. "I entirely forgot about that."

Dir angled his face away. He had forgotten it, too.

"Dir." She touched his elbow, making him start. She held the dagger tip-downwards in her other hand. "Teach me to use the knife again. I think I'm ready this time."

Gingerly, he turned the dagger point-up and closed her fingers around the hilt, his pulse hammering. He guided her knife-hand through the motions, showing her where to strike. His gaze fell to her lips, which were perfectly curved and full like ripe fruit. He let out a long exhale, dragging the tip of her knife across his bicep. How many times had he thought about kissing her?

"Show me where to strike," he murmured when he had shown her all the weak points.

Her hand trembling, she touched the dagger's tip to his arms and chest – wherever she could reach from this position.

"Good," he said, and she dropped her knife-hand immediately. "No one will be able to hurt you if you remember that."

She turned away, pressing her hand to her mouth. Dir stilled, unsure of what he had done. Then, she turned back to him. She held the dagger close to her breast. "Do you know why I killed my husband, Dir?"

He took a step back, shock and sudden anger flaring inside him. He could not stand the thought of Gennadiy Borisovich, the man who had won her, the man who had taken her. "I told you: I don't want to talk about your husband."

Masha pressed on. "He beat me. He beat me until I was covered in bruises and welts and my lip was split. Sometimes until I couldn't walk. He beat me every night and most days. I lived in terror for ten years. I prayed every night that he would kill me so that he couldn't hurt me anymore.

"He was paranoid and so kept the knives away from me," she whispered. "Without a knife, I couldn't use my magic. But Gennadiy couldn't stop the plants from growing. I mixed nunshood in his *shchi* and killed him, so he could never touch me again."

Dir was shaking. His former surprise had burned away by pure fury. If he could have killed Gennadiy Borisovich again, he would. Instead, he clasped Masha's hand over the dagger's hilt and said, "No one will be able to touch you like that again."

"No, they won't." She threw her arms around him, burying her face in his shoulder. "Thank you."

As his anger subsided, it was replaced by guilt. Dir had kept her knife away and thus had limited her ability to practice her magic. He gripped her shoulders and then held her at arms length. "You have the knife. Use your magic."

CHAPTER 10

Medny

The people of Medny watched Masha and Dir with suspicion and even ire. The first person Dir asked about the mountain spat at him. Most just shooed them away, muttering about ill-luck. Masha started hanging back, sensing that someone was watching her and certain it must be a too-curious townsperson. The wet snow falling throughout the day did not help Masha's mood or paranoia, causing gooseflesh to pucker along her skin. Finally, she and Dir returned to the Bloodmine Inn, no wiser about the mountain, its curse, or its maze than they were before.

The innkeeper slammed two mugs of *kvass* onto the table. "You two look sadder than two drowned rats."

Charming, Masha thought, grabbing his mug.

Dir gave the man a flat stare. "What do you know about the mountain and its curse?"

"Not another treasure hunter." The innkeeper looked like he was about to spit. Fortunately, he kept his saliva to himself and stomped away.

Nursing her *kvass*, Masha waited until the innkeeper was busy wiping down tables on the other side of the dining hall. She watched him carefully for signs that he might be eavesdropping. It was better than looking at Dir. Every time she looked at him, her heart beat quicker and she started to sweat.

"Medny sees lots of treasure hunters," she said quietly. "And the townspeople don't like them."

"I need to find out more about what to expect in the mountain," Dir said. "I thought they would know."

She caught a glimpse of him from the corner of her eye. His white-blonde hair, done in an elaborate braid down his back. His firm jaw. His sculpted shoulders. She stared at her reflection in the mug. *When* had that skinny boy from her memory turned into such a handsome, well-built man?

He was also *better* than she remembered. Last night, Dir had given her a way to defend herself and he had also let her summon a witchfire right in front of him. She had never been able to use her magic so … openly. If knowing how to defend herself was freedom, then using her magic in full view was triumph. Masha wasn't sure she had ever felt as powerful as she had the night before.

She felt bold.

"If the innkeeper won't speak," she whispered, "maybe the *domovoy* will."

Beyond the next table, a healthy fire crackled. Within the flames, she saw a sooty-black creature squatting, its large head on its knees. The *domovoy* blinked its ember-like eyes at her, perhaps surprised that she could see it as easily as it could see her.

Standing, Dir set his mug down with a thud. "I'll distract the innkeeper."

Masha hurried over to the next table, sitting on the bench closest to the fire. She held out her hands and pretended to warm herself.

"*Ved'ma*," the *domovoy* said in an almost childlike voice. "I thought your kind were hunted and killed for sport in these parts."

Not for sport, she thought as an image of the charred pyre and *ved'ma* flashed through her mind. She glanced towards Dir, who was speaking in a harsh tone to the innkeeper. She didn't have time to correct the spirit. "What do you know about the spirit that lives in the mountain?"

"You want to go to the mountain?" The *domovoy's* eyes widened to the size of plums, sparks flying. "The Lady of the Mountain is not easy to frighten or control. She is very dangerous for a human to cross."

"We are looking for a treasure inside the mountain," Masha said. "Is there a way around the … Lady?"

The *domovoy* shook its head. "You must pass her trials, or she'll kill you."

That sounded terrible, Masha thought. Would Dir change his mind? "What are the trials?"

"I do not know," the *domovoy* said. "But there is a man who has passed them."

"Who?" she asked. "Where do I find him?"

"Shemvuy Shumat," the spirit said. "He lives with the Old Ones on the eastern slope."

Masha bowed her head in thanks, splashing some *kvass* on the hearth for the spirit, before stopping Dir from upsetting the innkeeper any further. She and Dir retreated to their room, where she told him what the *domovoy* had told her.

"We will find this Shemvuy Shumat tomorrow," Dir decided. "I can't go home empty handed."

We'll be dead, she thought.

They retreated upstairs to their room, where neither spoke and they eventually slept. Masha dreamt of strange shadows climbing the walls, but every time she thought they were real, she woke up in a sweat. By the time the sun peeked through the window, she was exhausted but restless and ready to leave.

They left Medny in the early morning, heading uphill and eastward as the sun stretched long, orange rays across the gray-brown earth. As they climbed, they found snow clinging to the mountain, turning the path slick with ice.

After struggling up a particularly steep slope, Masha said, "I might be able to use a rune to melt the path."

Dir shielded his eyes. "Won't it turn it to mud?"

She considered her repertoire of runes and then shook her head.

"Try it." He shrugged.

Drawing the silver dagger, she pressed its tip into the ice and it sunk easily into the surface. She carved the rune for *kamy*. Stone. The path shuddered. Withdrawing her dagger, she sunk it into a different place and carved the rune again. The ice cracked over and again until the cacophony was almost deafening. Then, small stones emerged from between the cracks, settling atop the ice and creating a textured coating.

Masha felt warm and golden inside. Yet again, she had used magic in plain sight – and Dir wasn't shouting for her to be burned.

Dir raised his brows. "That's creative."

"It wasn't exactly what I planned," Masha admitted, standing. "I can only command the magic to begin, not what becomes of it."

He examined the path with an unreadable expression and then proceeded. With pebbles and gravel underfoot, they climbed upward with relative ease. As they crested the slope, a heavy, gray cloud rolled down the mountainside, bringing a freezing drizzle along with it. Masha groaned, blocking her face with her arm. Dir took the brunt of an icy gale, his cloak whipping around him. He took her by the arm. She forced herself not to freeze. His grip was firm, not rough. She was safe.

She trusted him, she realized with a pang in her stomach. When had she last trusted someone?

"We need cover," he said as the rain turned to hail.

He led her down a gravelly slope, their boots skidding. And then, he pulled her under a crooked rock overhang. There was barely enough room for two people to crouch. Masha pressed against the earth behind her, searching for space that didn't exist. Dir shifted closer, away from the falling ice. She felt every inch where they touched. His arm against her shoulder. His thigh and hip aligned with hers. His breath, steady and warm.

She swallowed. Their closeness only served to remind her how … appealing … Dir was. What might it be like to straddle those thighs, to have those arms wrap around her? She tried to distract herself with the minutia. His cloak was of the drabbest, scratchiest wool. His white-blonde hair was falling out of its braid. The knuckles on his right hand were white from clenching his fist too tightly. She bit her lip. Her attempt at distraction didn't work.

Why did she want him now, when she had already ruined any chance?

She shifted, futilely trying to put space between him and her duplicitous body.

"The storm will pass soon enough," he said, noticing her discomfort.

A wet snowflake landed on her lower lip. She brushed it off. Dir watched that movement like it was a threat.

CHAPTER 11

The Stone Flower

When the hail turned to snow and the wind calmed, Masha followed Dir back out onto the mountain. They trudged two miles across slithering mountain paths, the sun racing towards the western horizon. Then, Masha spotted sheep dotting the hills, shepherded by women in colorful clothes. She and Dir followed the sheep down a gradual incline, coming to a ring of stone houses. Inside the ring of houses, six wooden poles were erected – each carved with a face and a rune. Masha tried to make sense of the idols as she approached, the sun vanishing behind the mountain.

"You followed us." A shepherdess in an olive-green *rubakha* and rowan-red coat stopped them before they entered the hamlet, setting the butt of her walking stick firmly in the snow.

"We're looking for Shemvuy Shumat," Dir said as the sun disappeared. "We heard he has met the Lady of the Mountain."

The shepherdess turned her walking stick in her hand. "What makes you think that?"

Masha kept her magic close to her chest. Including the fact that she could see spirits. But she sensed that, if she did not speak plainly, this shepherdess would send them on their way. And if Dir found the Ancestral Crown, Masha told herself, she would earn a cut of the coin. Enough, surely, to make her way to Beluvod, where she would not be burned for her magic.

"A *domovoy*," she said. "It lives in the hearth at the Bloodmine Inn in Medny."

"Vile place. Deluded people." The shepherdess spit. Then, she tilted her head, examining Masha more closely. "You're a witch."

Dir began putting himself between Masha and the shepherdess, but Masha said, "Yes."

"I am too." The shepherdess rolled up her sleeve, revealing long-healed runes carved into her arm. "Except we do not call them 'witch,' but *julan moštêšo*. Wise women."

Masha clutched her chest, fearing her heart may have stopped. She inched closer to the woman. The runes were foreign to her, nonetheless she sensed their magic. What spirit had taught her these? Or were these runes passed from mother to daughter, sister to sister like magic was meant to be? Masha's mother... She wouldn't have taught Masha magic, even if she knew how.

"How many of you are there?" she asked.

"Half of us. Maybe a little more," the shepherdess said. "The mountain is magic and it mingles with our blood."

Dir shifted from foot to foot, his hand on his sword hilt. He was watchful, and Masha hoped that he would not act as rashly as he had with the *ovinnik*.

"We do not usually allow Ruthenians into our homes," the shepherdess said, rolling down her sleeves. "But we do not usually meet Ruthenians who are *julan moštêšo*. I will ask Shumat whether he wishes to see you."

Dir sighed and looked at Masha, who in turn nodded at the shepherdess.

The woman climbed the rest of the way down the hill, while Masha and Dir waited. Masha pulled her coat tighter around her throat. The air was colder at this elevation, and the snow clinging to her hair did not help. Breathing deeply, she imagined a fire.

Dir swung his cloak around her shoulders.

She blinked at him. "Aren't you cold?"

His face was bright, raw from the elements, but he shrugged. "I'm warm from walking. I'll tell you if I want it back."

They fell back into silence until a man traversed the distance between them and the Old Ones's hamlet. He was a short man – shorter even than Masha – with gray-hued skin and curly brown hair; and he was bundled into clothes just as colorful as the women. Stopping short of Masha and Dir, he appraised them with expressive hazel eyes.

This was Shumat, guessed Masha.

"You visit me like friends," Shumat said. "But I do not know you."

"I am Dir Olegovich and this is Maria Tarasovna," Dir said. "We were told that you have met the Lady of the Mountain."

"By a *domovoy*, I'm told." Shumat inclined his head. "I must admit I am surprised to meet a Ruthenian wise woman, and intrigued that she would assist a treasure hunter."

Dir was as still as stone.

"Dir made me an offer I could not refuse," Masha said. "And he has sweetened the deal since."

Shumat looked skeptical but said no more on the matter. "I will invite you into my home – to extend welcome to a wise woman and because it is not safe to traverse the mountain in the dark."

"What's out there?" Dir gripped his sword hilt, his knuckles turning white. When Shuman narrowed his eyes at the gesture, Dir released the sword.

"Nothing to worry about if you are inside." Shumat started down the hill.

He lived in the southernmost house, which was a simple one-room structure where he had a bed and a hearth. Masha was certain that all the Old Ones had similar layouts. However, Shumat boasted an array of mason's tools and stones, many of which were carved into almost lifelike sculptures. She reached out and ran her fingers across the smooth stone of daylilies, half-expecting them to be real.

Dir was uninterested in the sculptures. "I need to enter the mountain, and I need to come out alive."

"A greedy heart will not get you far in the Lady's realm." Shumat set a pot to boil and then began pulling root vegetables from a shallow cellar dug into the floor. "The Lady will test your heart. If she deems it unworthy, you will not return to the surface."

"She blessed you," Masha said, tracing the lip of a giant, granite thornapple. "With the ability to manipulate stone."

"I could already manipulate stone." Shumat chuckled as he chopped the turnips and carrots. "She gave me the ability to make it alive."

She inhaled sharply as the stone thornapple quivered beneath her touch. She felt no magic, though. Like the granite was truly a living thing.

Dir crossed the distance between them and grabbed her hand, his expression inscrutable. "She has a maze," he said to Shumat. "How did you make it through alive?"

"You know more than you should." Shumat scooped the vegetables into the boiling water. "The Lady blessed me and I should not reveal secrets she wishes to keep. But I can tell you my story.

"I always worked with stone," Shumat began, revealing a foreign rune tattooed onto his wrist. "I made beautiful creations – homes and idols of the gods. But I was never satisfied. So my father told me to seek the Lady of the Mountain, who grew flowers out of stone. I was a fool and listened to him. I faced the Lady's trials and passed them. That is when she came to me. The Lady showed me a malachite flower. It was more beautiful than anything in the world. Then, she told me to return to my home and give beauty to my people." He gestured to the stone flowers blooming all over his home. "When I returned, I could sculpt more beautiful things than I had ever imagined."

Masha realized that Dir was still holding her hand. He wasn't doing anything, just holding it midair. Her cheeks traitorously heated, and she pulled her hand away.

"She can be benevolent," Dir murmured.

"I was disillusioned when I went to the Lady," said Shumat. "I'm proof that you do not need to be a perfect person to be blessed by her."

Masha had never heard of someone surviving the Copper Mountain or its haunting. "How many others have been blessed by her?"

Shumat shook his head. "None I have met."

She looked to Dir, hoping that he would see the folly in his plan. He said nothing, refusing to meet her gaze. She unfastened his cloak from around her shoulders and then handed it back to him. She was plenty warm in Shumat's home.

CHAPTER 12

Peridot

Shumat and the rest of his folk rose before the sun. Shumat turned to sculpting, while the other men set to do repairs around the hamlet and the women let the sheep out to pasture. Bundling Masha in his cloak, Dir led her down the mountain as the sun rose and the snow glittered a thousand colors – a mirror of the sky.

"Dir," Masha began when the Old Ones were out of sight. "Why do you need the Pervaya Korona? There are other ways to earn money."

You don't have enough money to take care of me.

"Not 5,000 *grivna* worth," he said.

Dir refused to admit to her that he wanted the 5,000 *grivna* so that no one would say that about him again. He could give Masha 1,000 *grivna* and still be wealthier beyond his wildest dreams. Maybe then he could find a woman. She just couldn't remind him of Masha.

"We could die in that mountain," Masha said. "Is 5,000 *grivna* worth it?"

"I need to take care of Askold," he said. "He's my brother. He's worth … anything."

"If you die in there," she said, "Askold will have no one."

He stopped and turned. Her nose and cheeks were red from the cold; and she was holding his cloak tight around her. He wished she would hold him that tight. "You are afraid."

"Dir, you bought my bond and threatened to out me as a *ved'ma* if I did not help you." She looked around as though she might find someone to corroborate her story. "I would never do this of my own choice. And of course, I'm scared. I don't want to die."

He let out a long exhale. He had done so much wrong this time around. "I need your help. I don't know what to do with spirits and magic. And I know there will be some in that mountain."

"It's too dangerous."

He had always had a soft spot for her, even before he knew that a boy could love a girl. After all this time, it seemed like that tenderness was still there. "I will go alone if you promise me you'll wait in Medny for one week. Give me time to make it through the maze and find the Ancestral Crown. I owe you enough *grivna* to make the journey to Beluvod."

Her expression tightened, and Dir wished he could read her mind. The thought of losing her again made his throat ache and chest constrict. But if he continued to force her hand, he would never truly know what she thought of him now.

If she didn't still consider him too poor.

"I'll wait a week for you," she said finally.

"I will make it back alive and with the crown."

He held out his hand to help her down a precarious section. When she had climbed down the gravelly slope, she held his hand just a touch too long. Like he had when he had stopped her from touching the stone flowers. His heart thumped harder, hoping uselessly that touches meant something to her. They meant the world to him.

They continued down the mountainside, sticking to the textured ice that Masha had created yesterday. Lost in thoughts about the softness of Masha's fingers, Dir walked in silence; and Masha was uninterested in interrupting his rumination. After two hours or so of trekking, a set of bifurcated hoofprints. Dir was a soldier, not a hunter or tracker, but he knew these belonged to a small deer. Nothing that he thought he should worry about.

But as they rounded the sharp corner of a switchback, he put his arm out to stop Masha.

"It's a roe deer," she said.

"Roe deer are brown," he replied.

Thirty or so paces ahead, a small deer-like creature nuzzled the snow. It was the normal size and shape of a roe deer – two ears, four legs, wide eyes, and short – but this deer wasn't quite right. Its hide was misty gray and it wore five-pronged – not two-pronged – antlers. One of its hooves looked like pure silver.

"It doesn't *look* like a spirit to me," Masha said.

Dir didn't trust an anomaly like this – not after facing an *ovinnik* and a *vila* already. "Then, what is it?"

The creature raised its head and looked at them, its ears twitching. Then, it burst off in a spray of snow, bounding westward across the mountain.

Dir and Masha did not give chase, instead picking their way down the path. When they reached the place where the gray roe deer had been, they discovered swathes of rough, black stone rippling alongside the path. Like moss, raw peridot grew on those black stones.

Dir bent and touched one of the olive-green formations, wondering if he could "harvest" the gemstone and sell it elsewhere. "If it wasn't a spirit, it is an odd coincidence it was near this peridot."

"The shepherdess said that the mountain's magic affects the Old Ones's blood," Masha said. "Maybe it affects the animals too."

"A witch deer," he muttered, straightening. "Never thought I'd see that."

Masha laughed, and he loved the sound. "If not for the cursed mountain, I would almost like it here."

Dir had always lived in the Duskhollow slum in Vecherny. What would it be like to settle on a mountainside? *This* mountainside. With magical neighbors and a powerful spirit living below his feet. If Askold liked it, and if Masha wanted to stay... He bit the inside of his cheek and forced himself to keep moving downhill. Masha did not want to stay. Not with him.

CHAPTER 13

A Hot Bath

Masha sparred fist to fist with Dir in the privacy of their room at the Bloodmine Inn. Her skin crackled with energy each time they touched – a brush of the hand here, a graze of a shoulder there. It did not help her keep her head, and she grew winded faster than she should have.

Dir was the first to back away, holding his hands up. "In a few weeks, you'll be able to manage most opponents."

She couldn't help but smile. She knew how to shred a man's flesh with a knife; and now she was learning to defend herself with only her body as a weapon. That only made her buzz even more with excitement.

He passed her a mug of *kvass*, which she gulped down.

"I'll be headed to the mountain in the morning," he said, and her stomach dropped. He rummaged in his belt purse and then held out four *kuna*. "There's a *banya* down the street. It will be awhile before I get another hot bath, so I am going. I'm sure you would like a bath and a hot steam as well."

Masha could almost see that rye stalk of a boy inside him – eager, earnest, and asking her to join him on a sojourn. Truly, though, an adult man stood before her. Handsome and scarred by life. Maybe both her old friend and this new Dir wanted her to join them. She nodded, her throat too tight to speak.

"Come, then." Dir tucked away his copper coins and then made swift work of his breastplate and bracers.

Dir looked so different when he wasn't encased in leather. Yes, he was just as tall and broad, but he did not look like he would imminently butcher someone. When he disarmed, leaving his sword next to his pack, he looked almost relaxed. He caught her looking at him, his iron-gray eyes burning hot like a forge.

Masha turned away.

Leaving the inn, they walked a short distance down the slushy street to the *banya*. A shadow in Masha's periphery caught her attention, but when she turned to look, she saw nothing there.

The entrance room was small and divided by a curtain, with men undressing to the left and women to the right. Hanging her clothes on a hook, Masha stared at the wood paneling rather than the thin, patterned curtain separating her and Dir. Then, hurriedly, she let herself into the washing room.

The room was dark and smoke-filled. At its center sat a large, oblong tub made from wood, where a dozen or more women sat and chatted. Masha slipped into the water, hissing as it scalded her skin. But Zorya's tits, it felt good for her tired muscles. She slowly sank neck-deep into the water and closed her eyes, listening to the gossip. No one spoke to her, but that was fine. The fewer people she spoke to, the less likely someone would realize she was a *ved'ma*.

After a long soak, Masha went towards the back of the *banya*. She covered herself with a linen wrap and then stepped into the corridor beyond. Ceramic pipes ran overhead, bringing heat to the washing rooms. In front of her was a series of doors that led to saunas.

She picked one and found herself with company.

"Masha–"

"Dir–"

A stove burned in the center of the room, pluming black smoke towards the hole in the ceiling. Sunlight filtered in, dancing across Dir's torso. Masha staggered closer. A large, puckering scar started at his shoulder and twisted down his chest and to his hip. She reached out to touch him.

He caught her wrist. "Don't."

Her throat went dry as she met his gaze. With his thumb, he stroked against her pulse, making her nipples tighten beneath the linen. The wrap was a flimsy thing, and she wondered how much he could see.

"What did that to you?" she breathed.

"A Nyemetsky." He pulled her closer. "He cut through my armor. I was lucky he was just far away enough that he didn't kill me."

She licked her lips. "Very lucky."

They were so close – her standing between his legs. She could smell soap and leather and sweat. She could see the gray striations in his eyes. He made circles against her pulse, which made her entire body hum with anticipation. She wished she was wearing more – and less. She inched forward.

"Masha," he croaked, "don't."

"Don't what?"

She settled her free hand on the place where his shoulder and neck joined. His muscles tensed and released beneath her hand. Then, he pressed his palm against her lower back. She tipped forward and into Dir, a hot flush spreading across her face and chest.

Then, she dipped her head and brushed her lips against his.

Dir wrapped his arms around her and held her tight as he tilted his head back, deepening the kiss. He tasted like birch sap and salt, like iron and lingonberries. Masha scraped her fingernails against his chest, ran her palms across his muscled shoulders. Groaning, he held her tighter. His fingers splayed across her back, inciting a burning shiver to climb her spine. One of his hands found her breast, thumbing her nipple through the fabric. His gaze burned forge-hot as she whimpered and ground her hips against him.

"Tell me to stop," Dir said. "Tell me you don't want me."

She clasped his hand tighter to her breast, shaking her head. "I want you, Dir."

"Zorya's blunt teeth," he snarled.

He grasped the front of her wrap and tugged. The linen fell away easily, and then Masha was naked. Palming her ass, Dir dragged her forward and caught her nipple in his mouth. She gave a shallow, pleasured cry as he sucked, clutching his shoulders. Grinding her hips against his, she urged him on. He suckled and kissed and nibbled her breasts until she saw starbursts in her vision.

"Get up," he said. "Hands against the door."

As Masha obeyed, she heard his linen wrap fall to the floor. Then, he leaned against her, one hand pressed against the sauna's door. Her breath came out in rasps, her heart hammering in her throat.

"Do you want me?" Dir rasped. "Tell me. Now."

She spread her legs. Right then, she wanted nothing more. "Yes."

Masha gasped as he pressed inside her. He was larger than she had expected, stretching her in a way that made her legs go weak. Gripping her hip with one hand, he moved in and out of her with excruciating slowness. She dug her nails into the wooden door and moaned. This was nothing like Gennadiy's fast and awkward sex. Dir pressed kisses against her shoulder as he fucked her. No, Dir felt amazing, driving her higher and higher with each measured stroke.

"It feels so good," she whimpered.

"I can make it even better."

He slid his hand between her legs, his fingers forming circles over her clitoris. She bucked against him. The pleasure was undeniable, flowing through her in hot waves. She murmured his name as he buried himself to the hilt inside her; and Dir shuddered.

"I have wanted this for years," he breathed.

That made her pleasure spike. She leaned her forehead against the door. Her pleasure was like a *zmey*, flying and coiling and breathing fire inside her. Sweat streamed down her neck and back. Her hair clung to her face. And the steam roiled around her, caressing her nakedness like a second lover. She bit her lip. She was so close. When her climax hit, her legs buckled. Dir held her and she held on to the door as white-hot pleasure seared through her veins. She cried out, shaking. His arms around her, his cheek pressed against her back only made the pleasure better.

A moment later, Dir finished inside her with a low, animalistic groan.

They remained tangled together, leaning against the door. Dir let his fingers trail down her side and kissed her shoulder. Masha closed her eyes, relishing the feeling of being cherished and not used. It would only last a few more moments before she faced the reality that Dir would head to the mountain and she would not.

CHAPTER 14

The Malachite Maze

After the *banya*, after Masha and Dir returned to the inn, Masha brought Dir to her cot. They fucked once before sleeping and once in the middle of the night. Masha reveled in the simple pleasure of sharing her body, the satisfaction of hearing his moans of pleasure, and the contentment of lying with a man who strove to give her pleasure. She also admitted that she enjoyed Dir's heat next to her as she slept. She felt safe.

As orange and pink sunlight slatted through the window, Masha woke and stretched. Dir sat on the edge of her cot, lacing his breastplate on the sides. She sat, letting the blanket pool around her hips, and helped tie the laces for him. He gave her a hungry glance and then turned away.

"Stay," she said.

"I have to get the crown," he said quietly.

"Dir, I don't want you to die."

"I won't," he said. "I promise to return. You'll have your *grivna*."

She bit her lip. She did not care about silver. She wanted her childhood best friend to live. She wanted the man who did not shy from her magic and who gave her pleasure to live. And he wouldn't, not if he entered the Copper Mountain.

He stood, belting his sword and then hoisting his pack onto his shoulders. "I will be back within the week."

Masha was silent. He wanted her to stay in Medny, to wait for him. But this might be her best chance at escaping to Beluvod, to be safe from the witch hunters. If she waited, he would want her to return to Vecherny to collect the prize with him. Then, she would be more than a hundred miles from the border and right under the Princess's and her witch hunter's thumbs. From here, the border was only a day's walk.

"You will be here when I return, yes?" he said.

She turned away, in case he could read her intent on her face.

He sighed quietly and went to the door. "I hope you will be here."

She let him leave, her chest aching. When she no longer heard the sound of his footsteps, she dressed and tied the silver dagger to her belt. On the side table, Dir had left a handful of *kuna*, which she transferred into her pocket. She waited a while longer, running her fingers over the coins in her pocket. Then, when she was sure that Dir would have left the inn, she left the room and climbed down the stairs.

A few treasure hunters huddled in the far corner, but otherwise the inn's average visitors were merchants or copper miners who had yet to find permanent housing in Medny. The pinch-faced innkeeper offered Masha *kasha* and clotted cream, but she refused, having no appetite this morning.

Stepping out into the soot-covered streets, Masha oriented herself. *Eastward.* Beluvod and its holdings lay eastward. She would go that way. She took her first step, her stomach in knots. Part of her wanted to stay and wait for Dir. She reminded herself that would only lengthen her quest for freedom. And she had never planned to be with a man again, especially not Dir. So, she put one foot in front of the other until she put Medny behind her.

But worry and guilt ate at her until she felt hollow inside. She looked over her shoulder at the mountain. Was Dir inside it? Or was he still climbing? He did not know runes or how to interact with spirits…

Masha glanced around. In all directions, winter rye slept beneath a thin layer of frost. But no one else was in sight of her. So, she climbed off the path and into one of the rye fields. Drawing her dagger, she carved into the dirt *zri*, to see. Whether this rune tricked the eye or truly created a floating mist before her, she was not sure. But on the surface of the mist appeared Dir climbing the mountain through a snow storm. His boot slipped on ice and he skidded, catching himself on a jutting stone. Then, he disappeared and the mist showed her a crevice in the mountain, obscured dead leaves and fallen snow. *The entrance.*

"He'll never find it," she muttered as the mist dissipated. *Unless I show him.*

Scuffing dirt over the rune, she turned back to the mountain. Her stomach hardened with anticipation, but at least she knew what she had to do. She started back the way she came. She walked half an hour westward and then took a southern path up the mountain, hoping that this path would lead her to Dir. When the regular path ended, she took a goatpath upward and found the snowstorm Dir had been fighting. Snow fell in white clumps as she climbed, threatening to turn to hail or sleet. She curled her hands into her sleeves. It was brutally cold up here; and the wind did not help. She also dared not go any faster, lest she slip and fall.

Eventually, she spotted a brown cloak fluttering in the wind.

"Dir?" she called.

He turned, his consternation turning into surprise. "What are you doing here?"

"You need my help," she said.

"I know," he admitted quietly, reaching out his hand. "I'm glad you came."

"The entrance into the mountain is just ahead. There." She pointed.

A wisp of steam curled from between the rocks. Holding her hand, Dir guided her across slick stones towards the steam. He kicked away fallen rocks and fallen snow. Against the side of the mountain rested a half-buried stone slab. It wasn't what Masha had seen in her vision, but she was certain it was the same place.

"*Bogatstvo, likhoimaniye, likho.*" Masha traced the runes

carved into the slab. "Wealth, greed, misfortune."

"Sounds like what we're looking for."

Setting his jaw, Dir hauled aside the slab, revealing the crevice Masha had foreseen. It led into a narrow and sloping passage.

Masha would need to bow her head; Dir would likely need to crouch or go on his knees. Dir entered first; and then Masha entered the cold, damp space. It was dark and smelled of iron. Gripping the back of his shirt, she followed him down for what felt like eternity until finally her feet found flat ground. Fumbling in the dark, she scraped her knife against the stone floor and a weak fire sprang to life.

They stood in a small chamber, its floor covered in bones. She recognized those of deer, chickens, sheep, and even a human skull. She reached for Dir, and he took her hand. In the far corner, a set of stone idols – they resembled the idols from Shumat's village – leaned against the wall. Dead candles, bowls of rotting berries, and a few shining coins sat before the idols.

Her stomach felt like stone, but she said, "Leave an offering."

Dir's expression was unreadable as he fished a *kuna* from his beltpurse and tossed it at the grim idols. Then, he led her towards a dark mouth in the cave wall.

They navigated the next passageway by the flickering light of Masha's witchfire in the last room. Bones brittle from decades underground crunched beneath their boots. Dir squeezed her hand, and Masha didn't know whether she was grateful for his presence – or disgusted at herself for joining him here.

But she remembered the rye stalk of a boy she used to know.

And she remembered the man who had kept her from freezing, the man that watched her magic without judgement, the man who touched her like a lover.

How could she leave either one behind?

The corridor ended in front of another slab. In the dark, Masha could not see the runes, but she knew they were there. She traced them with her fingers several times until she knew what she was reading. "*Labirint' malakhitov'*," she said. "The malachite maze."

Dir moved this slab and then took her hand again, leading her through a passage that glittered darkly with crystal stalactite. Beyond that passage was a vast, echoing chamber. Crouching, Masha searched blindly and then found a rock the size of her palm. Carefully, she carved the rune for fire onto the surface of the stone. Again, the *vila*'s dagger cut through stone like butter. A purple flame erupted along the surface of the stone. It was cool to the touch: witchfire didn't burn flesh.

Ahead stood a silver arch inlaid with egg-sized pieces of polished malachite. Beyond the arch, a narrow passageway ran until it took a sharp right.

The maze.

"The story of the Beloved's Name says the girl was trapped here with her people's treasure," Dir said. "She waits for someone to know her true name. Then, she'll give up her treasure."

"Do you have any idea what it might be?" Masha asked.

He shook his head. "I hope there's a clue somewhere down here."

Maybe he was right. Raising her witchfire, she saw the walls beyond the silver arch, which were covered in runes. Some, she recognized. Many she didn't. Her breathing shallow, she stepped through the arch. Nothing happened. She tried to make sense of the runes. It did not seem to be a sentence or a pattern – not that she could discern.

Dir followed behind her, a hand settling on the small of her back. "We go forward until the path branches."

They went forward and then right and right again, walking down a long and silent corridor until the path diverged. They could go forward or turn left. Masha examined the runes.

"*Zoloto*, gold," she read. The runes arched and swirled as though handwritten, not carved into black stone. "*Z'miya*. Snake."

"Like the story about the Great Snake," Dir said. "A giant snake that knows where ore deposits lay. But it brings moral corruption – greed and strife – with it."

Masha shuddered. "I have no desire to see a giant snake."

Dir smiled briefly. "Agreed."

"Then, we try the 'gold' route?" she suggested.

"That's as good a plan as any."

Avoiding the "snake" route, Masha and Dir took the straightaway. They followed the path as it turned, folding back on itself several times. Though she knew that they continued to march forward along the path, Masha felt as though she was passing the same place over and over. She kept reading the runes for fire, root, and wind over and over again as she and Dir turned right and then left again. Then, they came to another malachite-studded arch. This one was covered in runes written in script so small that Masha could barely read it.

"Beware the gold," she translated. "May it burn you black."

CHAPTER 15

He Who Trusts Not

Dir and Masha had only made it a few steps past the silver arch when the arch vanished, leaving them in a particularly dark part of the maze. Masha held her witchfire up, but the purple light barely penetrated the darkness. Dir's hairs stood on end, and his heart thumped hard but slow. A place that resisted illumination.

He reached out until he found the smooth wall. It was uncomfortably cold beneath his fingers. "We can follow the wall."

Fumbling, Masha stepped in front of him and found the wall, too. They carefully proceeded forward – too close for Dir's comfort. She smelled like lilies, and her hair shimmered gold, red, and brown in the dim light. Dir wanted to thread his fingers through her hair, to kiss her neck and her shoulder. Watching her grope ahead of him, he thought only of their coupling in the *banya* and then the inn.

Dir had dreamt of taking her since he was seventeen or eighteen. Even after she repudiated him and married Gennadiy Borisovich, he fantasized about her more than he should have, though eventually –to his relief and regret – he began to forget about her. Now, though, he felt every ache and yearning that she had caused all those years ago. He wanted to fuck her again. He hoped that she would let him once they found the Ancestral Crown. Then, perhaps, it wouldn't be the desperate and needful fucking from last night. Maybe it would be easy and confident.

Is Beluvod where you want to go? he wanted to ask her. *So you can be safe from the witch hunters?* He wondered if Askold would agree to travel all that distance.

Masha looked over her shoulder as they turned a corner, and he glanced away. He should not plan a future with a woman who spoke nothing of one. If she no longer cared about his poverty, then she surely cared that he had forced her to accompany him.

They turned another corner and stepped into a low-ceilinged chamber where Dir had to bow his head. Masha lifted her witchfire, turning in a slow circle. The walls looked like water – shiny and rippling black rock – and white marble pillars stood in each of the corners. Dir tried to make sense of it, but couldn't. This was the Lady of the Mountain's creation, and it defied human understanding.

"It's a dead end," Masha said.

Dir took a deep breath. It was a maze; of course, there were dead ends. "We can head back the way we came."

"Wait." Masha approached one of the pillars and then crouched beside it, holding her witchfire torch close. "There is writing here."

"What does it say?"

"*He who trusts not proceeds not,*" she said.

"What does that–?"

Beside the pillar, an arch appeared in the rippling black stone. Wordlessly, Masha proceeded; and Dir followed quickly after her. They stepped into a cave-like chamber with thick, sandstone stalagmite jutting up from the floor. Above the same watery black rock ran across the ceiling. And somewhere further into the cave, water ran.

Like a match hissing to light, a red-orange flame danced across the nearest stalagmite. Dir blinked several times. The flame coalesced into a woman the size of his fist with red hair, alabaster skin, and a sapphire-blue *rubakha*. She stood on one foot and twirled, dancing and dancing. Masha staggered backwards and into Dir. He wrapped an arm around her as a sudden heat built in his groin.

The dancing spirit stopped, her limbs flickering with flame. "You seek treasure."

"Yes," Dir said.

"I can show you gold ore," the fire fairy said.

He shook his head. "I'm looking for a crown."

The spirit frowned, and his heart stuttered. Was he offending it? Speaking too rashly, like he had to the *ovinnik*? Then, the spirit shifted back and forth on its tiptoes. "You must meet the Lady, then."

Masha spoke then. "How do we find the Lady?"

The fiery spirit gestured onward. "Remove your weapons, and then let the river take you down."

Dir stiffened. "We need–"

"The pillar. *He who trusts not proceeds not*," Masha interrupted. "We have to … trust … her."

The spirit smiled sadly, which did not instill confidence in Dir.

Masha, though, had strode ahead as though drawn by an invisible hand. Her witchfire illuminated a rolling river, its waters sparkling black and purple in the firelight. She set down her magical torch and then untied the silver dagger from her belt.

She turned to him. "What are you doing?"

His throat constricted. He had not removed a single item. "I don't think this is a good idea."

"Trust the maze." She held out her hand. "And trust me."

He glanced back. The fiery spirit was gone, the chamber darker than it once was. Turning back to Masha and the river, he took her hand.

She pulled him close, her breasts brushing against his breastplate. His groin filled with an aching heat. She slipped the knife off his belt, then she unbuckled the strap that held his sword to his back.

Dir instinctively reached for her, but she slipped away, stepping right to the river's edge.

"Don't you want the *vila*'s dagger?" he asked.

"The pillars in the chamber said if we do not have faith," she said, "then we won't get any further in the maze. You want the crown. I want to make it out alive. I'll leave the knife."

He took her hand. "We jump on the count of four."

CHAPTER 16
The Doorless Room

Dir recalled nothing from their journey down the river, only that he woke up in another chamber where no water ran. The stalactite overhead glowed faintly. He would have thought the previous chamber, its fire fairy, and its river were a dream – if not for being soaked. Brushing stray hairs out of his face, he pushed himself into a seated position. Ten yards away, Masha lay, her dark hair fanning across the stone floor. She was unconscious but still breathing.

He went to her.

She woke at his touch with a start, her wide eyes searching for danger for a painful moment. He held his breath. Where was the woman who had fucked him in a public sauna? He thought that she was no longer afraid of him. He had really hoped she wasn't.

You're beautiful, he wanted to say but wasn't sure how she would react. Instead, he said, "You were right. I think. We seem to be deeper in the maze."

"In a doorless room," she said.

"Another challenge," he guessed. "I'll look around."

He searched the floor and walls, but found nothing. No runes, no signs of a doorway or window, no seams. Nothing. Was the puzzle to find a way to escape? He turned to her.

"Is there something I'm not seeing?"

She padded along the perimeter, opening and closing her mouth several times. Coming back to the place she started, she frowned. "I *feel* someone else's magic, but it's not here anymore. It's like … a residue."

"Is it hiding the exit?" he asked.

"I wish I had that dagger." Masha touched the wall gingerly. "A rune or two might show me what is here."

Dir walked the room again. In one of the corners, he found a pile of stones. He brought her a sharp rock. "Can you scratch a rune?"

"I'm supposed to carve." She tested the stone's weight. "But maybe it'll work."

Grimacing, she pressed the stone against the polished wall. The rune was faint, but it did appear. She scratched a second one immediately after the first. Nothing happened. Muttering something under her breath, she wrote the two runes again.

Then, Dir was alone. He spun around. Gone. Masha was gone. Had her runes freed her, but left him behind? He felt a sharp pang in his chest. She couldn't have *planned* this. There was no way. She didn't know what lay in the mountain. She didn't know there would be a doorless room that only she could escape from. He pressed his hand to the faint etches on the wall. Surely, she had not wanted to leave him behind.

"Dir."

He would recognize that voice anywhere. *Masha.* But it wasn't his Masha. It wasn't the Masha that he had bought out of prison, the one who had traveled from Vecherny to the Copper Mountain. That was the voice that had haunted his nights for years, the voice he couldn't escape. He turned.

Masha – young Masha – stood before him. She wore a green dress with orange embroidery at the neckline and a *panova* layered overtop. Her golden-brown hair was braided into a crown on her head and laced with flowers. When he looked at her, she flushed and her eyes widened.

"I didn't expect you to be here," she said.

You're too young. You're older now, he wanted to say. But his voice had other plans. "I had to come. I need to talk to you."

She bit her lower lip and looked at her shoes. "Maybe I should go. My parents told me I shouldn't talk to you."

"Please," he said, though he did not want to say the words.

"Don't marry Gennadiy Borisovich."

She looked at him. Innocent. Confused. "Dir, my parents want me to. And Gennadiy has a farm and a steady income. It's a better match than a girl like me usually gets."

"I don't want you to leave," he protested. He knew where this was going, and he did not want to witness it. Not again.

"I'll miss you, too, Dir," she said. "But you can come visit me."

Dir remembered shaking his head at this point. He didn't now. He seemed to have control of his body, but the maze forced him to speak. "That's not what I mean. I-I-I... Masha, I want you to marry me."

Young Masha staggered backwards, almost as if he had slapped her. Dir never had. She glanced around as though looking for something, her face turning bright red. "I, uh, I mean, my parents want me to marry Gennadiy Borisovich."

"But I love you," he blurted. "I've loved you for as long as I can remember. You can't marry him."

She patted her *panova* over and over, refusing to meet his gaze. "The wedding is ready to proceed."

"Please, call the marriage off. Marry me instead."

"I can't," she said.

"Why not?" His voice began to rise.

"I told you: Gennadiy Borisovich has a farm and a steady income from it. He'll be able to take care of me."

"I'm going to join the army," he said. "I'll have a salary, and I'll make sure to send it back to you so you can use it while I'm gone."

She shook her head wordlessly.

And still he pleaded, "It'll be enough, I promise. Marry me. I'll make you the happiest woman in the world."

"I can't," she said again.

"Why not?"

"You– You don't have enough money to take care of me," she said. "A soldier's pay isn't enough, Dir. Even your father's Varyag salary can't get your family out of the slums. I need something better."

It was only then that the enchantment let him go. Dir spun back to the wall, slamming his forearm against it and then burying his face in the crook of his elbow. Remembering that day was bad enough. Reliving it was enough to destroy him. He forced himself to breathe, repeating over and over that it wasn't real. He couldn't live the same moment twice.

CHAPTER 17
Obsidian

The rock hit the floor with a sharp *crack*. Masha was alone in the chamber, Dir vanished. Her hands trembling, she traced her etchings. *Zri, skryti*. See, secret. That should not have sent him somewhere. She didn't know a spell powerful enough to … transport … people or objects. So, where had he gone?

"Dir?" she said, hoping that he might simply be invisible, that her seeing rune had backfired when etched and not carved.

There was no response.

Pressing her back against the wall, she breathed deeply. Navigating this maze was *his* venture. *He* wanted the Pervaya Korona. Not her. But now she was trapped in this room alone with no apparent way out. She shouldn't have come back. She should have continued on to Beluvod. She drummed her fists uselessly against the wall behind her. She would have been nearly to the border by this time.

"How do I get out?" she asked the empty room.

The walls shook, and Masha staggered back. Their gray surface rippled, transforming into polished obsidian. Her reflection stared back from each wall, its eyes wide and skin pale. Then, the reflection began to warp. Dir appeared in the reflection. And though Masha stood alone in the chamber, the obsidian showed her and Dir in an eager embrace. Her skirts were hiked up around her waist and Dir was– She turned away, her cheeks burning. Another wall showed Dir striking her across the face. Trying to back away from that image, Masha stepped on the hem of her *rubakha* and fell. On the third wall, she knelt with her hands clasped in front of her as Dir walked away. The fourth revealed Dir with another woman. The reflections smeared into new visions. Cold partings, passionate embraces, cruel domination, and sweet touches.

She heard her name. She turned and found another image. Her face was bruised. Dir held her wrist too tightly, and she cowered before him like she had Gennadiy.

"No," she whimpered. "Please, not again."

She pressed the heels of her palms to her eyes. Her cheeks were wet. She was scared. Scared that Dir would be the same as Gennadiy. Scared that Dir *wasn't* the same as her husband and that she had made the worst mistake of her life. Scared that he would not want her. Scared that any moment might be the end with him. She had already lost him once, and she did not want to lose him again.

Wiping away her tears, she looked up. The walls showed only her ragged, slumped reflection. And floating in the center of the room was a silver archway, leading to a new part of the maze. Masha did not know what challenge she had passed, but she climbed to her feet and stumbled through the archway.

The silver arch opened into another part of the maze, this part distinguished by malachite walls and blazing torches cradled in silver sconces. Masha's shoes scuffed against. rough grooves in the floor. A rune. Bored into the malachite stone as though drawn with a claw. But what sort of claw could cut through malachite? *Z'miya*. The rune for "snake." The hairs on the back of her neck stood up. She had already seen that rune in the maze, and she was certain it wasn't coincidental.

Across from her, another silver arch appeared and Dir lurched through.

Masha clutched her chest. He was safe, and she wasn't alone.

Dir threw his arms around her. "It's you."

She stiffened, remembering the visions the obsidian walls had shown her.

He stepped back quickly, holding his hands up. "I'm sorry. I was just–"

"It's fine." She stepped back, suddenly fearful of his size. How did a man get so tall and so muscled? He could break her cheekbones with one punch. She shook her head, trying to banish the fear. She knew him, she trusted him. Zorya's tits, she *wanted* him.

"I'm just glad you're safe," he said.

Safe? She almost laughed. The maze had just shown her her worst fears. How was that safe? Instead, she nodded. "I was worried about you, too."

He offered his hand, and she forced herself to take it. *He who does not trust does not proceed,* she told herself. He had trusted her enough to shed his weapons and jump into a river because she knew the fire fairy was telling the truth. She had to trust him, even if the maze sowed doubt in her mind.

"What is that on the floor?" he asked, and she told him. He stilled. "I don't think a snake can carve a rune."

"It means 'snake,'" she insisted. "What else do you think it is?"

"*Zmey,*" he said grimly. "A dragon."

The ground vibrated, causing malachite pebbles to dance across its surface. And somewhere in the distance, a great rumble emanated. Then, far to their right, a tunnel of flame shot into the dark abyss above them, burning brighter than sunlight.

"I don't have my sword," he growled.

"You can't fight a *zmey,*" she said. "Run!"

They fled down the corridor until it forked. Her instincts took her left – away from the dragon. The vibrations shook the maze a moment. Grabbing her arm, Dir pulled her down another path. Behind them, a bright red flame spiralled. Masha gasped. They would have been incinerated. He jerked his chin. *Forward.* She nodded and then they hurried on. They took another left and then barrelled straight. She glanced over her shoulder. Dir ran after her.

Behind him, the *zmey*'s eyes glowed like furnaces. Its massive, scaly body scraped against the green stone walls. It shouldn't fit in the maze, but the walls warped to accommodate its bulk. It growled, the sound shaking the corridor so strongly that Masha lost her feet. Her shoulder struck the wall, and she didn't fall. Terror choked her vision as she pushed herself forward.

Dir was shouting. "Fire!"

He hit her, tackling her to the ground. A torrent of fire roared above them, the heat suffocating. She buried her face in his chest. Memories of being trapped and held down boiled towards the surface. She dug her nails into his leather armor. *This is Dir, my friend, my best friend, my...* She wouldn't have survived without him.

When the fire sizzled out, Dir pulled her to her feet. They followed the corridor as it veered right. The *zmey* rumbled, and chunks of malachite ceiling tumbled down. They dove into a narrow gap. Masha wheezed in the dust and smoke.

"Crawl!" he barked.

The corridor from which they came was gone, clogged by a thousand pounds of malachite. They could not go back. They couldn't resume their original path. Wiping the grime from her face, she started into the blinding dark.

CHAPTER 18
Violet as Witchfire

The passage emptied into yet another part of the maze. Masha collapsed against the far wall. The flickering torchlight and the relative openness was a godsend after fumbling in the claustrophobic dark. Dir crawled out shortly afterward, loose strands of his hair plastered to his face. Their gazes met, and then she fell into his arms. Broad. Muscled. Solid. At that moment, she felt so safe that she wanted to stop time and stay here.

The maze shook, and two burning eyes appeared beyond the torchlight. It was then that Masha knew that she would not escape this maze alive. Even if she had the strength to keep running, the *zmey* was too close. They could lie flat to the floor to evade its flame, but its teeth and claws would make short work of them.

It was over.

Dir untangled himself. "Hide in the gap." When she didn't immediately move, he snapped, "Go!"

As she scrambled back towards the way they had come, Dir stepped into the center of the corridor, his arms held wide.

"Look at me," he shouted over the *zmey*'s roaring breath. "I'm after your treasure."

The *zmey* clawed forward.

Dir staggered back, terror flashing in his eyes.

The beast opened its maw, its teeth like fetid stalagmites and stalactites. Masha couldn't move. Dir stood between her and the monster. Weaponless. The maze shuddered with the *zmey*'s growl. She was sure her heart stopped. This man would defend her against the impossible – and she was about to lose him.

The *zmey* pounced.

Masha covered her face.

But death did not come. Slowly, she peeked out from between her fingers. Trembling, Dir still stood in front of her, still willing to die so that she might escape notice. The *zmey*'s teeth clicked shut inches from Dir's face. Slowly – excruciatingly so – the monster receded, slithering back into the maze and disappearing beyond a shadowed corner.

Crawling out of the gap, Masha whispered, "Where is it going?"

He helped her to her feet. "I don't know."

"I called it back," said a third voice.

They both spun. Standing in the center of the corridor was a girl no older than thirteen. Her skin was as pale as alabaster; and her black hair, threaded with silver and copper, gleamed like polished obsidian. She wore what might have been a simple *rubakha*, save for that it looked as though it was fashioned from malachite and belted with gold. A green serpent wrapped itself around one of her wrists.

"The Lady of the Mountain," Masha said.

"You have come far." The girl looked sad – in the way a statue might look sad. "What wound made you seek me out?"

Dir was quiet for a moment, but then he said, "I am looking for the Pervaya Korona. I believe you have it."

The spirit looked sadder, disappointed.

Masha sensed that Dir's answer wasn't right. It didn't answer the question that the Lady had asked. She squeezed his arm. "Why do you want the Ancestral Crown?"

He opened his mouth, closed it, and then looked at her. Then, he said, "I need money to move myself and my brother out of the slums."

The Lady tilted her head, and Masha was certain that the spirit wanted something more. She squeezed his arm.

"Masha, I don't–" He shook his head. "I want the money because I want to prove that I can take care of my family."

Masha dropped her hand. He wanted the silver he might get to prove that he could take care of... *A soldier's pay isn't enough, Dir. Even your father's Varyag salary can't get your family out of the slums. I need something better.* She swallowed against the lump in her throat. He was risking his life because of what she had said when she was a stupid teenager?

"A man who is honest with himself is honest with the world." The Lady smiled then, sadly still, showing teeth like opal beads. "I will bless you, Dir Olegovich, with the strength of the mountain."

"And the Ancestral Crown?" he asked.

"There is one more challenge you must face," said the Lady. "You must tell me my name."

He hung his head. "I do not know it."

"I will give you a clue," the spirit said.

"*I slip through your fingers, light like air.*
Worth more than gold, copper, and silver.
I crown a pauper or a Prince just the same.
To ash I can turn, or I may burst into flame.

I work like magic, violet as witchfire.
I break, I mend, I rise above all.
What is the thing tugging at bards' lyres?"

Dir stared at the spirit, his expression blank. He reached towards his back, searching for a sword that was not there. He let his arm drop to his side. "I'm useless at riddles."

When he looked at her, Masha shook her head. She had known the answer to the *ovinnik*'s riddle so quickly. *Forgiveness.* But her mind faltered when she tried to parse this one. What worked like magic? Or applied the same to Princes and beggars? She shook her head. "I don't know. Maybe I'll think of it."

"I will give you one night in my mountain," the Lady said. "Find the answer, or be crushed beneath."

Then, the Lady was gone.

The torches dimmed, and Masha felt suddenly exhausted. She leaned against the wall and then slid down to the floor. She stared at the malachite floor, unable to meet Dir's gaze. How could she when she knew that her words had sundered something inside him? She had always hoped that he hated her because she had been petty and mean and not because she had struck something so deep that he spent a decade nursing the wound.

"Masha," he began.

"I'm sorry," she whispered. "I'm so sorry."

"We were young." He sat beside her. "Young and foolish."

"I was cruel," she said. "I proved that on my wedding day. You were right to be angry with me. You should be still."

He took her hand. "If we answer the riddle and we get the crown, would you stay with me? Me and Askold. We can go anywhere we want with 5,000 *grivna*."

Masha felt dirty. And not because she had been battered by a river, had crawled through rocks and dirt, and had nearly been roasted by a *zmey*. No, this was filth in her soul. A woman who would only be with a man because of his money. She had already done that, and that had given her Gennadiy. She wanted to be better for Dir.

"I should go to Beluvod," she said. "Maybe the *volkhv kniazhich* will have a use for me."

Dir said nothing, letting go of her hand.

CHAPTER 19
The Mountain's Warning

Dir paced deep into the night. Or what he thought was night. There was no sun or moon under the mountain. He repeated the Lady of the Mountain's riddle over and again. *I slip through your fingers...* But the moment he thought he had an idea, he thought of Masha. *Worth more than gold, copper, and silver...* She lay on her side, her back facing him, asleep. *I break, I mend, I rise above all.* He could not think straight.

They had made love in the sauna and then at the inn. He had let her stay behind, but she had chosen to accompany him. It all led him to believe that, this time, she would choose him. He hadn't even asked if she would marry him. Just that she would stay.

I should go to Beluvod. Masha did not ask Dir to come with her. He closed and unclosed his fists. If they escaped this mountain, he would even have silver. Enough to take care of her *and* Askold. That was what she wanted, wasn't it? The comfort and stability that money brought. He bit the inside of his cheek. This time, he would have it. And she still didn't want him. He turned back to her for a long moment, wondering what *would* convince her.

Enough, he told himself. He had mourned for Masha all those years ago. He didn't need to mourn her now. Not when his and her life depended on finding the answer to the riddle.

"What is easy to lose, worth more than riches, and is worn by Princes and peasants?" Dir muttered, circling around and around. He was no good at word games. "What can both break and fix and work like magic? And what do bards play songs about?"

Bards sang about adventures and heroes. He shook his

head. That wasn't it. Hammers fixed and broke things. Again, that wasn't the answer to the puzzle. Small things like pins and buttons were easy to lose; they could break and mend; and everyone wore them, at least. But were they worth more than riches? Dir would not say so. The longer he thought about it, he decided it must be an abstract concept, but his exhaustion slowed his thoughts to a standstill.

He sat on the floor, his elbows on his thighs and his head in his hands.

He heard a rustle. Masha was awake and had turned over. Dark rings under her eyes, she propped herself up on an elbow. "I didn't tell you what I saw in that doorless room."

Dir rubbed at the back of his neck, wishing he could forget that part of the maze.

"I saw ... visions," she murmured. "Of what our future might be."

He held very still. "None of them were good."

"Most were not," she admitted. "But... I think they were my fears. I was scared that you would be like Gennadiy."

That made him angry. He struggled to keep his voice level. "I will never raise a hand to you."

"I was scared that if you were not like him that I had ruined my friendship," Masha said, "and any hope to fix it."

Another heated emotion flared inside him. "I thought there wasn't. I thought I hated you. But I love you, Masha."

"Love?" She began to sit.

Dir was glad for the darkness. She could not see the deep flush across his skin. *Love her?* She had just rebuked him, and he still professed his love. Just like he had all those years ago. When he was a foolish teenage boy. He shook his head, at a loss for words.

Then, he realized it.

"Love," he growled. "The answer to the riddle is *love*."

The torches sparked and then blazed brighter. Dir climbed to his feet and then helped Masha up. The Lady of the Mountain stood in the middle of the corridor, her malachite dress shining eerily in the torchlights. She smiled, revealing her top teeth, as she scraped forward.

"Your name is 'love?'" Masha said.

"Yes," the Lady said. "I love the Old Ones, I love my Ruthenian husband, and I love the mountain."

In her hands appeared a simple crown made of copper that shone like blood, tipped in fiery gold. Its design was old – likely from a time before Ruthenia existed. Dir's palms itched to hold it, not just because it would bring him wealth beyond his wildest dreams but because the crown radiated with a power of its own. He stepped forward.

"In speaking my name, you have earned your treasure." The Lady held forth the crown in both hands. "Take it, Dir Olegovich, if you want it. But be warned that, in taking the crown, you will lose what you want the most."

He wanted the crown and the silver that came with bringing it to the Princess of Vecherny. He took the crown from the spirit, a shock of electricity coursing up his arms as he touched it.

"Thank you," he told the Lady.

"I hope your treasure brings you content." The spirit looked sad – if alabaster, obsidian, and malachite could look sad. "Go with my blessing, Dir Olegovich and Maria Tarasovna."

Another silver archway appeared in the maze. This one, though, opened to the night sky, the stars glimmering far in the distance. A chilly wind blew, carrying a dusting of snow into the mountain. Still clutching the crown like it might sprout wings and fly away, Dir glanced at Masha. Her expression was inscrutable. He wondered why. They had made it out of the mountain alive. Just like he had said they would. Wordlessly, he led the way through the arch and onto the mountainside.

CHAPTER 20
Divergent Paths

"I wish I had the money to celebrate." Dir sat on the edge of his cot, his fingers still wrapped around the Pervaya Korona. He hadn't let go of it since the Lady of the Mountain had given it to him. "But we'll have to wait until we get back to Vecherny. I will buy you as many rounds of *kvass* – and wine – as you want."

Masha watched the sun rise through the window. She could drown in alcohol, but she doubted it would fill the growing emptiness in her chest. There was something wrong with that crown, but Dir wanted it so badly and she was at a loss for what to say.

"Come with me to Vecherny," he pressed. "You've more than earned your share of the silver. You stopped me from making an ass of myself with the *vila*; you found out about the maze; and you read the ruins for me in the mountain. You did everything I needed."

All for that crown that he stroked with his fingers like a lover. He only wanted it so that he could heal the pain she had inflicted – and that damned thing was cursed or something. She could feel it. He wanted silver to prove to her, to the world, that he was worth something. She wanted to wrench the crown from his fingers and throw it out the window. Dir forgave her, taught her to defend herself, accepted her magic, and made love to her. He had been her best friend for years. He didn't need that crown and he didn't need *grivna*. She was the one lacking.

"The border with Beluvod is only a day's journey from here," she said. "I think it would be best for me to head that way. It'll save me time." *And please, don't keep that crown for any longer than you have to.*

"I will pay your way," Dir said. "From Vecherny to Beluvod. You can travel like a *boyarynya* in a carriage lined with fur."

Masha closed her eyes for a long moment. She deserved this. She was the one who had told him he was too poor all these years ago. Of course, he was trying to keep her by offering luxuries that he hadn't been able to afford before. But now, it made her feel cheap, greedy.

I love you, Masha. Why had he admitted that? All it did was hollow her out.

"Enough about where I will go. I will decide that later." She crossed the room and put her hand on the crown, which was uncomfortably hot beneath her fingers. "Put down the crown and fuck me."

His lips parted in something akin to awe as he stared up at her, but his fingers tightened around the crown. "Masha..."

She moved into his space, straddling his thighs. He inhaled sharply as she pushed him backwards onto the cot. Atop him, she wrested the crown from his grip and threw it to the floor. He moaned as though in pain, but then his hands slid onto her hips. Heat swelled in her belly. She would leave him tomorrow, but at least she could enjoy him today. And he didn't need to coddle that crown. He needed to hold her, so she could remember what he felt like when she was alone in Beluvod.

She pulled her *rubakha* off and let the cool air caress her naked skin. His hands on her waist were like brands. She relished them, memorizing the ways his calluses caught and caressed. She dipped down and pressed a hard kiss to his lips. His hands sunk to her hips, pulling her down against his erection. Letting out a low groan, she unbuckled his belt and pushed his tunic up and off when he lifted his shoulders off the cot. He ran his hand up her belly to cup her breast, and Masha gasped as he rolled her nipple between his fingers, sending hot bolts of electricity straight to her core. Clutching his shoulders, she ground against his hips, trying to burn away all thoughts of the crown. Of the maze. Of leaving for a second time.

"Zorya's teeth." Dir's gaze turned glassy, the nails of his left hand digging deliciously into her. "If you don't fuck me soon, I'll have to do something."

Dragging her fingers down his chest, she found the laces on his trousers, undoing them with an almost amateurish excitement. He was beautiful with those iron eyes and pale blonde hair, intimidating with his sinew and muscle. Inside him was a boy who wanted to protect his friends, and a man who did not flinch from her magic. Masha wanted him more now than she had in the *banya*. So when Dir rolled her onto her back and shucked his trousers and boots, she opened herself to him.

And yes, Zorya's teeth, his cock felt amazing as it slid inside her. She dug her nails into his back, drawing him in as deep as she could. "Fuck me, Dir, and make me come."

He made a sound like a desperate animal and then began to thrust – hard, deep, and so slow that it made her head spin. She wrapped her legs around him, moaned in his ear, and savored the feeling of him. Of being full, of lying beneath his wall of muscle, of touching his scarred skin. She pressed kisses to his shoulder and neck, her body alight with pleasure.

"I want you." Dir sunk dizzyingly deep inside her, and her toes curled. "I always have."

She raised her hips, offering him as much as she could give. "I want more."

"Anything." He fisted the sheets by her head, his rhythm wavering and then quickening. "I'll give you anything. Anything you want."

Masha's breath came out in rasps. She was close. So close.

Pressing his forehead to hers, he admitted again, "I love you."

Love. The word scalded. Worse when she was beneath him than when they were in the maze. She couldn't love him. Not when she would leave him a second time.

She bucked her hips against him, focused on burning away his admission. Like she had never heard it. Her pleasure peaked, and she buried her face in his shoulder, howling in ecstasy and agony. With a groan, he joined her, his whole body shivering as he lay atop her and cradled her.

When they had both caught their breath, he rolled off her and then pulled her by the hip to rest against him, chest-to-chest. He brushed stray hairs away from her face and then kissed her palm.

"I want this," he said. "Everyday."

If Masha was someone else, maybe. But she could not stay in Vecherny. She had hidden her magic her whole life, but if she just walked another day eastward, she wouldn't have to hide. And Dir deserved someone who he *knew* wasn't with him for the silver, who he *knew* loved him regardless. No matter what she felt inside, she had already broken their relationship.

"Masha?" he said softly.

She shook her head. "Let's not talk about this. Not now."

A muscle in his jaw twitched. Once she might have assumed he was angry, but now she read the hurt in his eyes. "I swear" – he took her hand – "I will protect you."

Masha closed her eyes. What she would give to have a man who *protected* her, rather than hurt her. She trusted Dir. She knew he would do as he promised. But how could she let him always wonder if he was only worth the things he could buy her?

"I know," she murmured. "But let's not talk about it now. Let's be happy that we found your crown and escaped the maze alive."

He pressed his forehead to hers and squeezed her fingers, falling silent. Masha sensed his concern, but she could not soothe him. They would go their separate ways tomorrow; he could not convince her otherwise. But for today, all she wanted to do was indulge in his leather-and-lye scent and languish in his arms.

CHAPTER 21
He Who Wears the Crown

Dir awoke to a cold cot. Running a hand over his stubbly jaw, he sat and faced the empty room. Outside, the sun had not yet risen and twilight still gripped Medny in its gray fist. His throat and lungs ached as he found his clothes, pulled them on. Masha couldn't have left too long ago. Her scent still lingered. Lilies. And the cot's mattress still held a shadow of her shape. Strapping his sword to his back, he resolved to find her. He had lost her once. He had to *try* to keep her this time.

His boot knocked against the Pervaya Korona. It glimmered like a ring of blood against the wood floor. He bent down and picked it up.

Along its surface, he found runes that he did not remember from the day before. Dir would have wanted Masha to translate. He still *did*. But strangely, he understood the runes. *He who wearest me becomest a Prince.* He ran his thumb across the engraving as though it might change the words, but they remained. A slight chill passed through him, and he found it difficult to think of anything but the crown and the runes.

Could he become a Prince? A Prince could dress his wife in the finest fashions – silk from Tang'an, lazurite from Makuria, and tigerskin from the eastern forests. He could offer her the finest wines from anywhere in the world and tantalize her with the best spices money could buy.

Dir realized after a long time that he was still standing in the middle of the room, clutching the crown. The sun had risen, spilling yellow light into the room.

He gnawed on the inside of his cheek. He needed to go after Masha.

His gaze fell to the crown in his hand, and his thoughts sank. *He wore the copper and gold crown as he rode a white horse across the fen, an army at his back. Ahead, a smaller army stood at the ready, waiting for their leader – a woman in red – to give orders.*

He shook his head to dispel the vision. Finally, he tucked the crown into his pack. He did not want to wage a war against the Princess of Vecherny. He just needed the silver she had promised. She could keep her throne and the crown.

Dir left the inn, spending the last of his coin to pay off their tab, and then headed eastward. Masha was certainly headed towards Beluvod, where *ved'ma* were not persecuted for their very existence. He did not blame her for wanting to go there. He just wished...

He who wearest the crown becomest a Prince, whispered a voice in the back of his mind. Dir faltered as he imagined disbanding the Princess's witch hunters, declaring *ved'ma* and other magic-touched humans permissible within Vecherny's lands. He could do that, if *he* was the Prince. If he put on that crown. He almost took off his pack and pulled the crown out before he stopped himself.

He had to focus on the task at hand: finding Masha.

After an hour and a half of walking, Dir crossed a frozen stream. Far in the distance, Beluvod's forest appeared – a row of dark, green trees topped with snow. Dir saw no sign of Masha, but he did notice a second set of footprints. He fingered his belt knife's hilt. Too large to be Masha's. Not old prints, but not made within the last hour either. A hawk circled ahead, having clearly spotted a vermin in the snow. Alas, Dir saw no man anywhere between the stream and the forest in the distance. He assumed that the man was another traveler.

The hawk overhead spiraled lower until Dir could see the white spots on the underside of its wings. But it did not drop. Perhaps Dir had spooked whatever mouse or rabbit it was hunting. After passing several times over his head, the hawk flew eastward towards the forest.

Dir's hairs stood on end, though he couldn't explain it.

He who wearest the crown becomest a Prince, the voice in his head said; and his concentration broke. He looked over his shoulder Medny was gone, though the Copper Mountain loomed in the west like a giant surveying its territory. Heat flickered to life in Dir's chest. What would it be like to lord over all that he could see? Dir shook his head. Assuming the Pervaya Korona belonged to the Old Ones, Dir wondered if their old royalty went mad from the crown or if this megalomania had been acquired under the mountain.

The crown urged him to turn around, to make the trek back to Vecherny where it promised he could be a Prince. He forced one foot in front of the other through the snow. He did not want to be a Prince, just a man wealthy enough to keep his brother and wife comfortable.

He slowed. *If Masha even wants to be my wife...* She would have stayed if she had. She would have returned to Vecherny. She wouldn't have left before dawn.

Dir felt the weight of the Pervaya Korona in his pack. He unslung his back and then pulled out the crown. It gleamed red in the midday sun, its edges burning gold. The runes seemed deeper now, more apparent. *He who wearest the crown becomest a Prince.* The crown willed him to wear it. He ran his fingers across it instead, a sudden warmth filling him.

Maybe Dir was making yet another mistake. He had forced Masha's hand, dragging her along on this journey. Now that she had upheld her end of the bargain – she had helped him acquire the crown – she no longer saw a need to stay with him. He grew hot beneath his clothes. He didn't understand how she could fuck him, kiss him, sleep against him – all while planning to leave him behind. But Masha had confused him before, abandoning their friendship to marry Gennadiy Borisovich. He shouldn't be surprised that she would set aside their rekindled ... friendship ... to go her own way now.

"I'll take you back to Vecherny," Dir murmured, tucking the

crown away.

CHAPTER 22
Lilies on the Windowsill

The forest looked almost like a painting, the trees smudges of blue, green, and white against the horizon. Masha stared at them and refused to look back, no matter that her chest hurt. She wished that Dir walked alongside her, but he wanted the Pervaya Korona. She wanted freedom. Freedom from fear of being discovered as a *ved'ma*, and freedom from her former mistakes. So long as Dir wanted to return to Vecherny and earn his prize, they were at odds. And so the Beluvodian forest was her destination.

A hawk with white spots on its red wings soared overhead, circling once and then disappearing. Otherwise, she saw no animal or man as she walked across the unused land between the Copper Mountain and the forest.

By midafternoon, the trees became real – birches, firs, and spruces. Masha estimated that she would reach the forest in another half-hour. Then, she would be in Beluvod. Then, she would not worry about being burned alive because of her magic. She imagined the city of Beluvod and its palace, where the Prince's son was a *volkhv*. She had always been under her parents' or Gennadiy's thumb, then pressed to perform Dir's task. Now, she was finally free to go to Beluvod. She hoped she could find work there, maybe even magical work.

A tickle coursed down her spine, and she glanced over her shoulder. She felt like someone was watching her. But only snow stretched out beyond her. Rubbing the back of her neck, she told herself that she was imagining things. She trudged on.

The last stretch was quiet, the breeze barely a whisper and her boots crunching softly through snow. She reminisced about the night before, her legs locked around Dir's hips. She prayed that she would remember forever how good he felt. The first time she had left him, she had been haunted by his hurt and anger. This time, she would have a happy last memory of him. One that would keep her warm on cold Ruthenian nights. One that would keep her company when she was lonely. She looked down at the embroidered gloves he had given her. She was blessed to have had this second chance.

As she finally reached the forest, she spotted the hawk again. It circled around and around as though hunting her. Pulling her coat tighter, she hurried into the protection the forest offered.

Lifting her skirts, she sidestepped roots, fallen branches, and thorny bramble. She expected birdsong, the chatter of squirrels, and the rustlings of other creatures. Instead, she was met with stillness. Did the other animals sense the hawk? She glanced upward. She did not see the raptor. Breathing shallowly, she forged her way further into the forest.

Masha heard a hiss, and then she felt a hard strike against the back of her shoulder. She fell forward. Struck the ground and knocked the air out of her lungs. The snow and earth turned red-black around her. She blinked, pain blooming across her back and chest. She tried to push herself up but her right arm was useless. She slumped back onto the ground. Just in front of her face, an arrow lay in the snow. Someone had shot her?

Dead leaves and snow crunched behind her. Masha craned her neck, her vision blurring from pain. A tall and thin woman with ice-white skin and untamed, brown hair approached. At her belt, she carried a length of rope and trinkets glimmering with silver.

"No," Masha groaned and tried dragging herself one-armed across the forest floor.

The woman – a witch hunter – pressed her boot to Masha's back. "I've been following you since Slomaniy, *ved'ma*. I tried to catch you, but you always had that big, ugly bear with you."

Masha cried out as the witch hunter pulled her hands behind her back and bound her wrists together. The forest spun. Masha closed her eyes, shivering from the pain. Zorya's tits, but she had *known* someone was following her. She should have looked harder.

"Please," said Masha, "let me go. I'm going to Beluvod. I'll never set foot in Vecherny's lands again–"

"Get up." Grabbing Masha's good arm, the witch hunter tugged her to her feet. "We're going back to Medny."

Blood spilled down the front of Masha's clothes. She wasn't sure she would make it back to town. "I'm losing too much blood."

The witch hunter dragged her forward. "If you die, it's one less *ved'ma* to steal children and curse our crops."

"I've never hurt a child, never cursed anyone." Her head spun as she stumbled alongside the other woman. "Please, you have to stop the bleeding."

"Shut up," the witch hunter snapped. "Or I'll cut out your tongue."

Masha clamped her mouth shut, wincing with every step. The witch hunter walked quickly, and Masha tripped on her own feet. The world flickered in and out. Her blood felt hot, pouring down her chest and back, but the rest of her was painfully cold. She forced herself to think of Medny's *banya*, where it was so warm and where Dir had been. It was better than thinking of the pain, the blood, or her imminent death.

Stepping beyond the forest, the hawk darted down, landing heavily on the witch hunter's shoulder. The woman hooded the creature and then continued to drag Masha onward.

The sun was setting, painting the snow purple and pink in an intoxicating combination. And with the disappearance of the sun, the world only grew colder. Masha shivered uncontrollably, her mind darting between thoughts so fast that she couldn't keep up. The Copper Mountain loomed, a darker shadow against a darkening sky. Suddenly, Masha wished that she had been trapped down there – or crushed. It would be better than this.

To Masha's surprise, she survived the walk back to Medny.

An exhausted, ghostly version of herself staggered onto the town's streets in the early morning, just as she and Dir had when they returned from the mountain. This time though, she did not feel triumphant. Nor bittersweet. She felt ... nothing.

The witch hunter brought her to an unornamented, two-storey building. Masha could not imagine the inhabitants appreciating before-sunrise visitors – especially one that would bleed all over their floors – but the witch hunter knocked boldly on the front door. A manservant with round, ruddy cheeks opened the door, clearly irritated. When the witch hunter announced her purpose, he nodded and disappeared back into the house. Moments later, two burly guards with sashes emblazoned with the Princess of Vecherny's sigil stepped outside.

"This one's the *ved'ma*," the first one – a man with moss-green eyes – said. "You might as well have left her to bleed out."

"If she's not burned, she'll come back as a revenant," the witch hunter said as Masha swayed on her feet.

The moss-green eyed guard sighed. "Better get the pyre."

Masha's legs buckled. "Please, I haven't done anything wrong."

The witch hunter clocked Masha on the side of the head. "Your *existence* is wrong."

No, *ved'ma* were as natural as *kikimora* and *ovinnik*. Masha was born with her magic, like she was born with her brown hair and eyes. But she had no more strength to speak. Blood speckled the snow around her knees.

The second guard passed the witch hunter a purse that jingled with coins. Then, the man took hold of Masha and hoisted her like a sack of grain over his shoulder. Black bursts filled her vision, and Masha almost vomited from the pain. The moss-eyed one disappeared back into the building, only to return with three more bleary-eyed guards. The witch hunter faded into oblivion as the guards brought Masha to Medny's center. In the town's center, the three extra guards piled bundles of sticks and firewood, while the moss-eyed guard and the one carrying Masha bound her to a heavy beam. Finally, they set her and the beam atop the kindling.

Masha closed her eyes, unwilling to watch the guards light her pyre. As smoke filled her nostrils and her world grew painfully hot, she envisioned Dir – a future that would never happen. An apartment, a set of runes carved into the doorframe, a box of poppies and lilies growing on the windowsill.

CHAPTER 23
Earth

Dir did not know what made him stay another night in Medny. Nor did he know what made him wake up in the small hours of the morning. Unable to sleep and haunted by the desire to don the crown, he felt like he was still trapped underground. He slipped from the Bloodmine Inn and into the streets. Some fresh, cold air might do him good. The stars looked like knife points hanging about his head, and he had a strong urge to return to the inn – and the Pervaya Korona. Scrubbing at his face, he quickened his step.

Dir smelled smoke and the faint scent of lilies. His chest constricted. Surely, he was imagining the lilies. Masha was well into the Beluvodian forest. Not anywhere he could smell her. But as he walked northward, the smell of lilies grew stronger. A smudge of smoke rose against the sky, blurring the stars. He frowned. The smoke was real. He walked towards it, catching a whiff of burning spruce and birch. And lilies, still.

He turned a corner and then saw it.

A pyre, burning like the sun in the dark of night.

His heart dropped into his stomach, and he reached for the sword he no longer had. *Masha*. What other *ved'ma* was here? He broke into a run. They couldn't burn her. She couldn't die.

"Stop!" he shouted.

"She's a *ved'ma*," said a guard.

"She's innocent," he said.

"Do you hear yourself man?" The guards drew their swords. "She's a *ved'ma*. Her blood is tainted."

Dir shook his head. "Let me pass."

"She's already dead," said the nearest guard.

It couldn't be. He clenched his fists. She *could not* be dead. "Move," he growled.

"By order of the Princess," said the guard, "we burn all *ved'ma*, *volkhvy*, and *koldun*."

Dir tried pushing past, but the guards leveled their swords. His breath came out in rasps. Just twenty feet away, the pyre burned with Masha atop. And he couldn't reach her.

"Move," he said, and when the guards didn't budge, his anger rushed upward like fire from a mountain. "*Move!*"

I will bless you, Dir Olegovich, he heard over the hammering of his heart.

In his mind's eye, he saw a rune. *Zemlya.* Earth. His arm raised of its own accord. His hand traced the rune in the air. The guards blinked at him. He stepped forward, unafraid. Then, the earth shuddered. The guards held their ground. The earth shook again. Then dirt and gravel and stone lifted from the ground, wrapping around the guard's legs like earthen vines. One by one, the guards toppled. Dir leapt over them and ran to the pyre. The rune appeared again. He wrote it in the air; and the earth climbed the pyre, smothering the pyre.

He climbed onto the dirt and ashes. Masha lay unconscious, strapped to a half-burnt beam. Without even a belt knife – having left it in the mountain – Dir pulled at the ropes securing her. They crumbled, more ash than fiber. Then, carefully, he lifted Masha into his arms, cradling her against his chest.

Dir knew he could not return to the Bloodmine Inn right then – not after attacking Medny's guards – and he did not have the supplies to head out back towards Vecherny. So, he turned towards the mountain. He jogged. Those he passed that ignored him, he ignored in turn. Those who tried to waylay him or cry out, he trapped in a coating of earth.

When he finally left Medny and made it onto the mountainside, he found a small outcropping where he laid Masha down. Her *rubakha* was black from the fire, her skin as well. Carefully, he brushed away the soot and ash. She was still breathing, if barely. He sighed. He wasn't too late. Then, he noticed the hole through her right shoulder. An arrow wound, by the looks of it. He tore the bottom of his cloak and wrapped her shoulder the best he could. She would need a physician – or another *ved'ma* – soon.

Another ved'ma.

He looked up the mountainside, remembering Shemvuy Shumat and the shepherdess. Both had magic. One of them, or one of their neighbors, might know healing runes like Masha did.

After a few moments' rest, he lifted Masha again and carried her up the mountain as the sun rose. He followed the same path they had taken just days before, passing the rills of peridot left behind by the strange roe deer. Without Masha's magic, the mountain paths were nearly impassible in the early morning when everything was frozen, but Dir would not let the mountain defeat him. Not when Masha's life depended on it. Eventually, he found the Old Ones's sheep, followed by the shepherdesses. He hiked down the same incline that led to the ring of stone houses and the ring of old gods.

Shumat – as short and gray-skinned as Dir remembered – greeted him with a solemn gaze. "Ruthenians hate magic."

"Can you help her?" Dir asked, his voice breaking.

"She is far gone," Shumat said quietly. "Jansula takes our worst cases. Bring your woman to my house. I'll find Jansula."

Dir brought Masha to Shumat's house, settling her on the ground near the hearth. Waiting for Shumat and the other *julan moštêšo* to return, he crouched beside Masha and continued to brush away the soot.

"When the Lady said I would lose what I wanted most if I took the crown," he said, "did she mean I would lose you?"

Because as he watched her chest rise and fall less and less, Dir realized: he didn't care if he had silver and he didn't care where he lived. Not if he couldn't share it with Masha. He loved her. He had admitted that. But he hadn't admitted that, after all these years, she was *still* what he wanted most.

"Stay with me," he murmured. "Just a little while longer."

Shumat returned with an average-built, monobrowed woman who wore her gray hair in a trio of braids. Jansula rolled up her sleeves. "They burned her."

"She has an arrow wound," Dir said. "It went straight through."

The older woman drew her knife. "At least I don't need to remove the arrow."

Jansula removed the shoulder and sleeve of Masha's *rubakha*, exposing the wound. She demanded rags and water, which Shumat dutifully provided. She cleaned around the wound. It was red and bloody, but if it had begun to fester, the fire had burned the infection away. Carefully, the older woman felt around the wound. Then, she pressed her knife into Masha's flesh. Dir turned away. He had watched Masha carve his own skin, but he couldn't bear watching Masha cut.

When he turned back, he beheld Jansula's work. The *julan moštêšo* had carved a necklace of runes across Masha's collarbone. Already, the arrow wound had begun to heal; and Masha breathed easier.

"She was nearly gone," Jansula said, standing. "These runes will need to be reinforced daily until she wakes up."

Dir stiffened. "How long will that take?"

"If she does not wake in six days," the older woman said, "then the gods have turned their backs upon her and she must walk the long road."

CHAPTER 24

A Honeyed Drink

Masha slept for one day, then two, and then five. With each passing day, Dir lost hope. By the sixth day, he wondered if she would die naturally from her wounds or if he would need to end her suffering. Rubbing his hands on his trousers, he prayed for the former. He did not know how he would survive killing her.

Shumat turned from his chiseling and magicking of stone. "The Lady blessed you."

When Dir blinked, he saw the rune *zemlya*, earth behind his eyelids. He nodded.

"What gift did she bestow?"

"A rune." Dir watched Masha's chest rise and fall minutely, willing her to wake.

"The Old Ones still honor theirs and the Lady's shared blood," Shumat said. "If you wish to stay with us, you may. We will teach you our runes."

Dir shook his head. "I have a brother in Vecherny."

"If you must return to Vecherny, do not take the northeast road back to Medny." Shumat lifted a small, stone chalice from his worktable. Made from granite, it was carved to resemble an open thornapple. "I will show you a path to the south and west. It is more circuitous, but you will avoid any guards or witch hunters who know your face."

"I'll leave tomorrow." He caressed Masha's cheek with the back of his fingers. She did not stir. "She has a few more hours before..."

"Before we know that she has taken the long road." His lips

thin and gaze downcast, the short man hugged his thornapple chalice close to his chest. "May the gods lead her way."

May Zorya bring the dawn, thought Dir, *and not the dusk.* He squeezed Masha's lifeless fingers. He wanted a new life with her, not an end.

Sliding off his chair, Shumat crossed the room to a shelf lined with ceramic bottles. He uncorked one and filled the thornapple chalice with a liquid that smelled strongly of honey. He offered the chalice to Dir. "We call it *puro.* It will make you feel better."

Dir wanted to be in agony so long as Masha was. But that was self-destructive. So, he took the *puro* and gulped the entire cup. The honey-tasted drink hit him like a stone to the face. He swayed on his chair and bent forward, cradling his face in his hands. He did not hear Shumat leave, but the next thing Dir knew, he was alone with Masha. And the earth rune hung painfully close in front of his eyes. But he was too drunk to raise his hand and trace the rune.

A small and pointed-nose woman climbed from the hearth. She trotted to Masha's side, tilting her head. She had chicken feet. A *kikimora.*

Dir shook his head, disbelieving what he was seeing. He dropped his head back into his hands, taking a deep breath. He could not see spirits. Could he? He had never thought he could trace runes and cast magic either. Maybe this was another gift from the Lady of the Mountain.

He didn't think long on the matter because he drifted off into a drunken sleep.

Dir woke up with a start. A hand – mottled pink and brown and white with half-healed burns – rested against his knee. His head pounding, he tried to make sense of the hand. He raised his head. Masha lay in Shumat's bed, her arm thrown out to the side. She hadn't been in that position when he fell asleep. Carefully, he took her hand, drawing a circle on her palm with his thumb. Her fingers twitched minutely.

"Masha," he croaked. "Can you hear me?"

For a long moment, she was still. Then, her fingers twitched again.

Dir moved closer. He cupped her cheek. "Come back, Masha."

She sighed, her brow furrowing.

"I wore I would protect you. I did," he said. "I'm sorry I was not there soon enough."

"I should not have left like I did." She did not open her eyes, and her voice was barely a whisper.

"I..." He swallowed. "I only care that you're safe."

Her fingers curled around his, and she was silent.

"We're with the Old Ones. One of their *ved'ma* helped heal you. We can stay here until you're better." Dir forced himself to say the next part. "And if you want to go to Beluvod, let me take you there. I left behind the crown, so I won't get any *grivna*. And I have to go back to Askold. But at least let me make sure you make it safely to Beluvod."

Her eyes slitted open. "I don't need silver."

He winced. The loss of the crown meant he would remain effectively penniless. He and Askold would have to find another way out of the slum. And Masha would move on to greener pastures.

"I'd rather have you," she rasped, "than all the silver in the world. I am sorry that I ever thought otherwise."

Dir exhaled slowly as a tightness in his chest he hadn't known was there loosened. He squeezed her hand, speechless.

"I'll live in Vecherny, in the slum," she said. "So long as you're there."

He still couldn't speak, overwhelmed with visions of a future he had thought he would never see. A home with Masha and his brother, lingonberry preserves boiling on the hearth, his sword put to rest atop the mantel.

"I love you, Dir," she murmured.

"I love you, too." He kissed her forehead. "When you are well, we will return to Vecherny. Then, you, Askold, and I will find a way to leave the slums. We can return here to the Old Ones, or we can go to Beluvod. Or anywhere else we'd like."

Dir wasn't sure how much she heard because when he finished speaking, she was asleep again. He lifted her hand pressing his lips to her knuckles. She had survived her burns and arrow wound. And this time – his third chance – he would *not* let her go.

CHAPTER 25
Vedmak

Over several weeks, Masha healed. The weather grew colder, the snow turning heavy and constant. The Old Ones corralled their sheep into their homes and bunkered down for the winter, sharing stories over crackling fires and cups of a strong drink called *puro*. Once Masha was well enough, she and Dir slept on sheepskin and wool blankets on the floor of Shumat's house each night, huddling together for warmth and comfort.

Some days, Masha watched the *julan moštêšo* use their magic, tracing the scars along her collarbone. The Old Ones had their own runes, completely separate from Ruthenian ones. They seemed, too, to be different on some fundamental level. When Jansula tried teaching Masha the Old Ones runes for water and ice, Masha could barely summon either – just a few droplets of water and a single thumb-length icicle. Jansula tried the Ruthenian rune for fire and only produced a few embers. While the women conferred about what might be the difference, they never came to a conclusion.

"Will you teach me runes?" Dir asked after Masha spent a day experimenting with Jansula. When Masha cocked her head in confusion, he explained, "The Lady of the Mountain gave me a gift."

He traced something in the air and then the ground buckled beneath her feet. She nearly fell, catching herself against Dir's chest. Where she had stood, a fresh column of earth – a few inches tall – protruded from the snow.

"You're a *vedmak*," she murmured.

"I only know one rune," he said.

"Write it in the snow for me."

"*Zemlya*. Earth," he said, brushing the rune away as the mountain shuddered.

"I've never seen that rune." Kneeling in the snow, she drew a rune. "This is stone."

"Show me more," he said.

So she drew him *og'n* or fire, *zri* or see, *skryti* or conceal, and *izlechivat'* or heal. Without a knife, her finger-tracings in the snow were ineffective. But the Lady had given Dir a stronger power. His first rune – *og'n* – made the snow burst into a small cyclone of flame that he put out with a shower of earth.

"I am glad my first attempts were not like that," she said. "I would have burned down my parents' house."

Shumat stood a few paces off, watching with his arms crossed across his chest. "It is the Lady," he explained. "She fuels Dir Olegovich's power, just like she fuels my artistry. It makes his strength superhuman."

"She blessed me with the strength of the mountain," Dir said, and Masha remembered the Lady bestowing that gift.

"The magic of the mountain," Shumat concluded.

"What is the mountain's magic?" Masha asked. "It has a maze filled with spirits and trials."

"It shifts and bends and changes what it is in order to protect," the Old Ones said. "For us, it has protected us, our treasures, our culture."

Dir lowered his head. "I should not have taken the crown. It belongs to the mountain."

"The Lady is our *kniazhna*. We are nothing without her, and she is nothing without us," Shumat said. "She knows the meaning of each treasure under the mountain. And she would not give what should not be given."

Dir met Masha's gaze. "The crown was cursed. It clouded my judgment."

The hair on her arms stood on end. She remembered how he

could barely look away. How she had to wrest it from his grip. "She blessed and cursed you all at once," Masha said.

"I deserved it," Dir murmured, stepping closer.

Masha felt a trill of desire deep in her belly. She had been too injured; and then they had been in too close of quarters with Shumat. They hadn't been intimate since she had snuck away all those weeks ago.

"No one deserves what they get," Shumat said, disturbing the moment. "Be grateful that her curse was easy to throw off."

The Old Ones walked away then, leaving Masha alone with Dir again.

Standing on her tiptoes, she kissed him on the lips and then settled back on her heels. "Dir–"

"I'm glad for her gift, even if it's too strong," he said, taking her hand. "It brings me closer to you. *Ved'ma* and *vedmak*. I can learn the fear and the wonder you have because of your magic."

"I could have taught it to you," Masha said. "I was too scared as a child. Then, I was a fool as a young woman. But now, I'm ready."

A slow smile came to his face. "I'm ready, too."

EPILOGUE

Leaning heavily on her walking stick, Masha followed the sheep back from their pasture and to their pens along with the other women. Each day that went by, her trek to and from the mountain pastures grew more challenging. She took a moment to catch her breath, letting the other women finish herding the sheep into the pens.

She rested a hand on her belly, which was swollen with child. A happy consequence of making love to Dir whenever and wherever she could.

Jansula came alongside her. "Go home. Soon enough, you won't be able to join us."

"I said I would work as long as I could," Masha said.

"Your witchfires keep us warm at night and you helped with lambing," the older woman said. "You have earned time to rest before your own lamb comes."

Masha nodded, not wanting to argue too hard over the matter. She *was* tired and constantly growing.

She crossed the circular village and returned to her home. She, Dir, and now Askold lived in a stone house that Dir had made with his magic. That spring, she had carved runes – a blessing for those who lived inside, a curse for those wishing harm – onto the door frame. And now that it was summertime, poppies and lilies grew in abundance around their home.

Dir came to Masha, pressing a kiss to her lips and then guided her to the table. She sat beside Askold.

"Shumat taught me how to carve thornapple faces," Askold said, showing her a block of granite carved on four sides with the flower. The man glanced at his brother. "He's trying to teach Dir how to use his magic with more … finesse."

"I have the strength of the mountain," Dir said. "And mountains don't have finesse."

Masha threaded her fingers with Dir's. "Jansula says the child will be a girl."

"Masha," Dir murmured.

"I thought we would name her Olga," she said, "after your father."

"What about Maria?" he suggested. "After her beautiful mother?"

Masha flushed, and Askold rolled his eyes.

"I do prefer this mountain village to the slums," Askold said. "But I really preferred Dir when he was more sullen."

Masha hid a smile.

"Focus on your masonry, not on me." Dir leaned down, his breath fanning against her throat. "I think Olga is beautiful, and I hope she is a *ved'ma*."

Her heart ached from joy. Dir was still a man who treated her like a lover and did not shy from her magic. And here amongst the Old Ones and on the slope of the Copper Mountain, he embraced his own magic. Now, he would welcome magic in their child. She brought his hand to her lips and kissed it.

"I love you, Dir Olegovich," she said. "More than all the silver in the world."

ACKNOWLEDGEMENT

This novella was a true challenge to write. For a very long time, I did not know what story - exactly - I was telling. That resulted in 3 failed drafts before I finally wrote the story that became The Malachite Maze. And now you have this novella in your hands.

None of this, of course, happened in a vacuum; and I have plenty of people to thank for their help in finishing this novella.

First, I would like to thank my husband (profusely) for allowing me to spend hours and hours after work and over the weekend writing. I am sure there are times he would prefer that I was doing something else, but he has always supported my passions. Without his support, I would not have been able to write and edit The Malachite Maze in 4 months and bring it to you only 3 months after publishing The Bone Doll.

Next, I would like to thank my beta reader, S.R. Dreamholde who helped me with both The Bone Doll and The Malachite Maze. Their reading and comments have been invaluable in bringing you the most finished stories I can.

Finally, I would like to thank my romantasy writing group. It is an honor to be able to be a part of such a dynamic and inclusive community.

ABOUT THE AUTHOR

Rebecca Ganesh

Rebecca Ganesh is the author and cover designer for the new romantasy series the Ruthenian Chronicle.

A professionally trained librarian, Rebecca spends their time gathering all the most compelling and erudite information to make their characters and world building pop.

Rebecca enjoys a good fantasy novel and is always on the lookout for new story ideas.

Get freebies, book recommendations, and behind-the-scenes looks at: https://rebeccaganesh.com.

BOOKS IN THIS SERIES

The Ruthenian Chronicle

The Ruthenian Chronicle is a romantasy series of 4 planned novellas, each centered on a different couple and based on Slavic folklore, and related short stories. These books work as standalones and can be read in any order.

The Bone Doll

Real heroes are made of blood and scars and wounds so deep you cannot see them.

Viktor needs to bring back magic that can control the raging forest spirit that threatens to tear down his family's estate. He learns of a bone carving that can bind spirits, he sets out to find it. When he finally finds the talisman – the Bone Doll – out on the eastern tundra, he learns that it can only be used by its bearer - a grumpy shaman named Syra who only begrudgingly agrees to help him.

Traveling southward with the nobleman Viktor, Syra finds herself away from home for the first time, carrying a talisman that may or may not be cursed. And to make matters worse, she doesn't know if her magic is strong enough to wield the Bone Doll and defeat the forest spirit.

As they navigate wilderness and civilization, the mundane and the magical, Syra and Viktor's feelings grow and change. But Viktor hasn't been entirely honest about this quest: this is a journey from which Syra won't return.

Perfect for readers who loved The Witcher, Spinning Silver, The Wolf & the Woodsman, and The Bear & the Nightingale who want a little more romance.

The Wooden Heart

"I would have never thought that a wooden heart would beat."
"Only for you."

Having settled affairs with his estate, Viktor returns to the tundra and to Syra. However, his and Syra's hopes for a long-term partnership and romance are jeopardized. Viktor reveals that he has been cursed by the vengeful forest spirit that had threatened to destroy his estate. He is turning into wood. Syra devises a plan to visit a magical island with ancient and powerful spirits who may be able to break the curse.

Will Syra and Viktor make it to the island before Viktor turns completely to wood? Will the spirits remove the curse? Or will the spirits demand too steep a price?

Perfect for readers who loved The Witcher, Spinning Silver, The Wolf & the Woodsman, and The Bear & the Nightingale who want a little more romance.

This short short story follow the events in The Bone Doll by Rebecca Ganesh.

The Malachite Maze

He had always had a soft spot for her, even before he knew that a boy could love a girl.

In prison for murdering her husband, Masha is certain that she will be sold to a slaver and shipped off to a foreign land to live her days in servitude. So when the jailer comes to get her, she is surprised that it is not a slaver that has paid her bail but her ex-best friend Dir - a man whose heart she broke years ago.

Dir needs Masha's help in looking for a magical crown. The Princess of Vecherny is offering a large sum of money to whoever finds the crown; and Dir wants to pay his way out of poverty.

And if Masha doesn't help him find the crown, Dir will reveal Masha's closest-held secret - a secret even more dangerous than murder.

The Malachite Maze is perfect for readers of The Witcher, Shadow & Bone, Spinning Silver, and The Bear & the Nightingale.